'What's wrong, Adam?' Becky asks.

'I think we should finish.'

'What?' she gasps.

'Yeah. I think you should go out with some-one else, someone who can take you out on Saturdays . . .'

'Adam, I didn't mean . . .'

'No, I want us to finish. That's what I really want.' The words are just ripping out of him now, tearing his insides as they go. And she's looking at him with such bewilderment, such hurt. The pain makes him shout. 'I've been wanting to end this for a while.'

'You have?' Becky can hardly speak. It's as if she's suddenly run out of air. All she can do is gasp, breathlessly. What's happened? What's gone wrong? Adam docsn't want to end it, does he? This isn't the brush-off, is it? But then boys are so cowardly about ending things. And their cowardice makes them cruel. The last boy she'd gone out with just stopped returning her calls. No goodbyes, no thanks for the good times. In the end it was his mum who told her, pity just dripping off her voice. She thought Adam was different from other boys.

*He is different . . .*

A panel of readers across the country are the first to see Pete Johnson's books. Here are their comments on book II.

'I like the way each chapter takes you deeper into the characters. I feel as if I know them as well as my friends at school – actually the characters in Friends Forever are nicer than most of my friends. The situations are ones we're all familiar with and can relate to.'

'I was reading this on the train and one part about Mark and his mum made me laugh out loud. Mark's mum talks exactly like mine.'

'I love Cathy, she seems like the best friend everyone wants. She's sensitive, sensible, caring and down to earth but she also seems a lot of fun. I wish she was my best friend (mine's just told me she isn't my best friend). Jason is also close to my heart. He's just like a boy in my class who everyone fancies. Becky is turning into a really interesting character.'

'The book gives off such an atmosphere, I can't wait for the next one.'

*Also by Pete Johnson*

Catch You on the Flip Side
The Cool Boffin
We the Haunted
Secrets from the School Underground
I'd Rather be Famous★
One Step Beyond★
Friends Forever I: No Limits★

★ available in Teens · Mandarin

FRIENDS FOREVER 2

# BREAK OUT

# PETE JOHNSON

Teens · Mandarin

First published in Great Britain 1991
by Teens·Mandarin
an imprint of Mandarin Paperbacks
Michelin House, 81 Fulham Road, London SW3 6RB

Mandarin is an imprint of the Octopus Publishing Group

ISBN 0 7497 0623 6

A CIP catalogue record for this title
is available from the British Library

Phototypeset by Intype, London
Printed in Great Britain
by Cox & Wyman Ltd, Reading, Berkshire

# Contents

Dedicated to Miriam Hodgson, hopefully an editor forever and Jan, Liza, Annie Dalton and Daren Rumble.


'Friendship, a shared dream, something the participants have to believe in and put their faith in, trusting that it will go on forever.'

*Raymond Carver*

11 Cumberland Avenue
CARTFORD
Thursday night

Hi,

I've been asked (told!!) to fill you in on *Friends Forever I*.

My name's Cathy, by the way – sorry, that should have come before. And the book's about six people (Jason, Mark, Lauren, Adam, Jez and me) who are the best of friends (well, most of the time anyway!). How did we become such good friends?

Well, we all live in the same village and we all went to Farndale School in the town. You wouldn't believe how much the other kids in the village hated us for doing that. One day after school, Mark, who is not very big (understatement) was caught by the posse, as the local kids called themselves.

So after that, of course, we went everywhere together. And if Lauren or I had to stay behind for a detention (!) or something two of the boys would always wait for us and then escort us to the hut. This was our own secret hiding place that no one else ever knew about.

As we got older, the aggro started to die down. But we still banded together, especially when one of us needed help. About a year and a half ago, Adam's girlfriend, Lisa, was killed in a car crash. I just felt so sorry for Adam and yet there was nothing I could say.

Then there was Lauren's fifteenth birthday party. Lauren and Jason had just started going out together steadily, though they'd fancied each other from the first day they'd met. Anyway, Jason turns up at Lauren's party with a girl no one had ever seen before draped over his arm. To this day I don't know what made Jason do it.

But Lauren just ran out of her own party and has been very *very* (note the emphasis) bitter about it ever since. She said she would never speak to Jason again and expected me, as her best friend, not to speak to him either.

I can't tell you how dodgy the next few months were. Luckily, Jez managed to avoid the whole mess by shooting off to Berlin for a year. (He's a year older than the rest of us.) When he returned we'd all left school and were getting ready to go to college to do A levels (except Jason, he got a job in the local sports shop) and Jason and Lauren *still weren't talking*.

I decided the feud had gone on long enough and I invited Jason to join us to celebrate Jez's homecoming. Not a good idea. You see, I didn't tell Lauren, and when she saw him come over I thought she'd combust. In the end she stormed off and went away with this guy, Grant, though not very far – his car wouldn't start.

Anyway, you'll never guess who Grant is, only our English teacher at college. And he's invited Lauren out for a meal at Lombards, a very swanky, stuck-up place. I told Lauren not to go with him but she's been in a funny mood lately. You see, secretly she's still yearning for Jason (she will deny this, but believe me, I know). And recently she's started getting these unsigned notes saying, 'sorry'. And I'm sure they're from Jason.

Meanwhile, Mark has become very friendly with a new girl called Becky. I think he was hoping to go out with her but it's Adam she fancies. So Adam's going out with Becky tonight, his first proper date for nearly two years. Mark's really pleased that Adam is going out again. In fact, it was Mark who really set the date up. He's been brilliant, especially as – well, it can't be easy for him, can it?

By the way, Adam hasn't told his parents he's going out with Becky, as his parents are strict Jews and believe he can only get serious with another Jewish girl. They've been introducing him to Jewish girls all year but Adam hasn't cared for any of them. Only Becky.

What about me? I'm busy planning an anti-meat demonstration outside Radleys supermarket where

I work. The demo will take place when the managing director visits.

There's so much more I want to tell you but I think I've waffled on long enough. I'm sure you'll soon get to know everyone. You won't see me in the first chapter (look disappointed) but you *will* see Lauren out with her English tutor. You may also meet Jez (who works at Radleys too). He is going round to Jason's to try and get him and Lauren back together again.

But first, meet Adam and Becky, out on their first-ever date. Aaah!

They're on the next page.

I'll see you soon. Take care.

Cathy. XX

# Two Love Letters, One a Fake

The lights begin to dim. And Adam's in agony. Not again, he thinks; they couldn't be that cruel.

But then there's a crackle and that voice again, oozing itself all over the restaurant: 'Ladies and gentlemen, it's also Veronica's birthday. She's twenty-nine again. Ho! Ho! And we'd like you all to join in and wish Veronica a happy birthday, so are you ready?'

One guy even calls out 'Yes', his brain clearly melted away long ago. And then the waitresses appear: one little procession bearing a cake and a drink with sparklers in it set off in search of their victim while all around the room other waitresses appear, swinging their arms with such fervour as to make your average cheer leader seem anaemic.

The waitress nearest Adam's table is particularly muscular. 'Can't hear you,' she calls.

1

'That's because we're not singing,' Adam mutters. Then he stares at Becky. She's just hating this evening, isn't she? In fact, this is probably the worst date she's ever been on. He glares up at the beefy waitress. It's all her fault. But the really shaming thing is, it's not her fault, well, not entirely. The meal was going dead, wasn't it, even before the first birthday sing-song?

Why hadn't they just gone for a drink? They could have circulated and broken things up a bit. But spending an entire evening trying to make conversation with a girl he'd only ever smiled at in corridors? He must be crazy.

Jason could do it. In fact, Jason always reckons that first date with a girl is the best because that's when they think you're really special. Jason hates it later on when, as he puts it, 'they find out the truth'. Adam knows that with him, girls have to wait for the good stuff. Perhaps he should have a slogan printed on his T-shirts. DON'T PANIC, I DO GET BETTER.

They're all clapping now. Adam leans back. He smells, reeks, of after-shave. At school when all the boys first discovered after-shave, great tidal waves of it poured over in assembly. It took hours to unclog your nostrils afterwards. Why had he splashed it on like a nervous eleven-year-old? He digs into his left pocket and pulls out a packet of polos. Mark gave him these to keep his breath fresh for afterwards. *Afterwards*. That's a joke. He's surprised Becky doesn't do a runner now while it's dark. She's still there, isn't she?

The lights go up. Becky smiles nervously at him. 'There can't be anyone else left with a birthday,' she says. But she wouldn't mind a couple more when she's eating her main course, she's so convinced she's going to dribble her food.

She sits in silence, exchanging anxious smiles with Adam. Tonight all those bits of conversation which normally keep flowing through her head have deserted her. When they first sat down she was just gibbering, talking such rubbish that she knew exactly what he was thinking: I'm out with a retard.

By the soup course she was telling herself to ask him questions, find a subject he'll enjoy talking about. She ended up firing so many questions at him it felt more like a job interview than a date. No wonder he hardly touched his soup. He's leaning back again now. He's got big arms and long shoulders. In fact, he's got quite a large face too – an open face. He's also got straight teeth, short finger nails and no wax hanging out of his ears (she always notices things like that). There's so much Becky could tell you about him, if only she could think what to say to him. Come on, say something, anything.

'Go anywhere good on your holiday this year?'

3

She's really scraping the bottom of the barrel. Next she'll be asking what he got for Christmas.

'Didn't go anywhere this year but a couple of years ago went to America.'

'Whereabouts?'

'Ohio.'

'How exciting – that's brilliant.' She's gushing now, 'That's really brilliant.' She's said that already. Ask him something about Ohio. But what? Her brain stalls again. 'Did you fly over?'

'Yes, that's right.'

'Oh brilliant.' Stop saying that.

'And – er – did you have a good flight over?'

'Yeah, very calm.' He looks as if he's about to say something else and leans forward. But in the end he just sniffs and leans back even further than before.

Come on, keep the questions going, 'And – er – how big was the plane?' As soon as the words dive-bomb out of her mouth she's blazing with embarrassment. Why ask that? No wonder he says, 'Pardon?'

Desperately trying to recover the situation Becky says, 'I mean, was it a big plane because so many things can happen to you on big planes, can't they? Well, they can on a small one too, of course. Only not as many because obviously there are more people on a bigger one . . .' she stops. 'Excuse me, but do you know what the hell I'm talking about?'

4

He sits staring at her uncertain how to react at first and then they both burst out laughing. They are still laughing and tears are spilling down Becky's face smudging all her mascara when the waitress arrives with more food. She gives them such a puzzled look they begin to laugh even louder.

Finally, Becky announces, 'I can't laugh any more, I've got a pain and I feel rather strange.'

'Strange,' echoes Adam.

'Yes, all giddy and light. Do you?'

'I do a bit, yes.'

'Why's that, Adam?'

'I don't know,' he grins, 'perhaps they put something in the air.'

And then the lights start to dim again. 'I know what's happening now,' cries Becky. Only now everything's funny, crazily funny. And when they discover that it's Derek's birthday this time, Becky has a minor coughing fit. 'Derek,' she gasps, 'I didn't think there was anyone left in the world with that name.'

'He's the last one,' says Adam.

Becky starts to laugh again. He smiles at her gratefully. He's never made a girl laugh so much as he has Becky, tonight. It's quite exciting really. And now their waitress is by the table slapping her thighs. 'Come on you two, sing up,' she urges. 'I couldn't hear you at all last time.'

Adam is just wondering whether it's worth pretending he doesn't speak English when Becky says solemnly, 'I'm sorry, but we can't sing tonight.

'Why not?' asks the waitress briskly.

Becky stares up at the ceiling. 'Because my dog died this morning.' She gives a piteous sigh. 'And my budgie's in a coma.'

Lauren gazes around her. She still can't believe that she is eating chicken kiev in Lombards, the most exclusive club for hundreds, if not thousands of miles around. And sitting opposite her is her English tutor, who is easily ten or fifteen years older than her. There are just so many other women he could have picked. She must be the only sixteen-year-old here tonight. Not that anyone could guess her true age. When she was twelve, she was already at least twenty-five in her head.

And never has she eaten in a restaurant with so many mirrors. There's one on every pillar and an absolutely giant mirror stretching across the bar and glittering so fiercely, she can hardly bear to look into it. Everything seems to gleam and sparkle, especially the army of perfect young men in shiny white jackets and black bow-ties, who just hover permanently around the tables. You put an empty glass down and within seconds one of the gleaming young men is depositing it in a basket. You stub out a cigarette in one of the glass ashtrays and almost before you know you've done it, the cigarette is noiselessly removed. It would all be most impressive if only one of them would smile occasionally.

The only people who smile here are the black and white movie stars on the walls, their faces frozen into giant grins as if to make up for the absence of smiles elsewhere. By chance, the movie star beaming her silverly laugh on them is Lauren Bacall. Grant tells Lauren about her famous namesake and at first she is interested. But he goes on far too long, something he rarely does in class. When he starts telling her which films to watch she nearly says, 'Is that extra homework then?' but has a feeling he wouldn't find that funny. Does he lecture his older lady friends like this?

Grant puts down his knife and fork and leans back on the padded seat. He has been eating trout with almonds, a real, 'I am older than you' dish, as you have to know how to get into it for a start, then how to eat it without choking on the bones.

'Would you like to see the sweet menu?' The guy who asks has his hair in a small, neat ponytail, just like Jason. Lauren had noticed him right away. The music from the dance floor suddenly becomes louder. If Jason were here Lauren could imagine him pulling her downstairs and just diving on to the floor. When they'd arrived, she and Grant had stood by the balcony watching the disco below.

7

But he said he didn't dance and she could tell he found the disco very boring.

Jason had always promised to take her here. He never did, of course, (he probably wouldn't have got inside Lombards). All he did was give her misery. No, that isn't true. There were good times too. And right now those good times felt so close. For he did send her those flowers, didn't he? She keeps trying to picture him going into that flowershop and buying those red roses. But that's hard, as Jason isn't the kind of person you imagine going into flowershops. Well then that proves how sorry he is. And that he still cares about her.

So what is she going to do? It's up to her now. She'll ring Jason. No, she'll arrange to meet him . . . but it seems rather mean to start planning a reunion with Jason when Grant is taking her out for a meal. She'll work it out later. It'll be something to look forward to.

She looks up. A woman in a ghastly leopardskin dress with a massive belt and thigh-high boots strides past their table and down on to the dance floor. And she's got a definite, 'I'm so special' air about her, like most people here. Lauren looks across at Grant and she realises he's seen her too. For most of the time, as Cathy says, Grant's eyes are just 'like splinters of ice', but every so often there's a kind of lightning change and his eyes start twinkling with amusement and fun. Like now.

'Grant, I don't know what to have,' says Lauren.

'Try the chocolate cheesecake. I can thoroughly recommend that,' says Grant.

'Chocolate cheesecake. Mmm. I can feel it clogging up my arteries already.'

Lauren looks up at the boy with the pony-tail. But his eyes remain as stone-like as ever. Jason would have laughed and flashed one of his wicked grins and when Grant wasn't looking probably asked Lauren for her phone number.

'All right, chocolate cheesecake it is,' says Lauren. 'I can see I shall have to go on a diet for a month after this.' And when the boy is out of earshot she says, 'Are they all programmed not to smile or something?' She points to a sour-looking couple on the table opposite theirs. 'They look as if they've just come back from a funeral.'

'Queen Victoria's, probably,' replies Grant. 'This is a terribly snooty place, no denying it.'

'This isn't really your scene, then?'

'That's a quaint sixties phrase you've just exhumed,' he says.

'What is?'

He wrinkles his nose. 'Your scene.'

In class Lauren might have got embarrassed, but not now. She continues, 'What is your scene? Let me guess: wine bars, jazz clubs, park benches.'

'Anywhere but here, actually.'

'But you seem to know this place quite well for

someone who hates it so much.' Lauren's tone is teasing now. But Grant doesn't seem to mind.

'Actually, I've always hated this place. It was my wife who liked it.'

'Your wife,' gasps Lauren, and then immediately regrets her shocked tone. It must make her seem so naive. But she'd never thought of Grant being married.

'By the way, my wife and I are separated,' says Grant.

Lauren's about to say, 'I'm sorry,' but then she fears Grant might pick her up on that. So instead she asks, 'Have you been separated long?'

'It was brewing for a while. Then last summer things got very complicated. So my wife left, taking our son Royston with her. My wife,' he adds by way of explanation, 'is an ardent feminist and supposes all women are treated as second-class citizens when, in fact, it is men who are currently suffering at the hands of women.'

'I wouldn't agree with that,' says Lauren promptly.

'I wouldn't expect you to,' says Grant. Even when talking about his marriage his voice remains flat and toneless. Yet in a way Lauren likes that.

Grant is one person who always seems in control of himself. That's part of his appeal. In class, too, nothing upsets him. No one's ever heard him raise his voice, let alone shout. Lauren can't help feeling

10

flattered by this burst of personal news. Especially as earlier he'd refused to give her any gossip about the other lecturers. He must trust her.

She's just savouring her last mouthful of cheese-cake when she gets a surprise. A girl with eyes like currants is staring across at her from the bar. And it's a girl from her English class. She's sure it is. But how did she get in? She hasn't even got an escort, she's just with another equally unremark-able girl. Then Lauren cheers up. That girl is just with a friend, while she is with their tutor. Lauren hopes it is the girl from her class. Then they'll all see the circles Lauren moves in. They all thought he liked Tricia Williams.

But then Lauren suddenly thinks of Grant. Would he get into trouble for taking a student out? 'Grant, you couldn't lose your job over taking me out, could you?'

Grant stares across at her. He has a habit of holding a gaze. He's doing it now. 'No, I couldn't,' he says finally. 'But it certainly wouldn't help towards promotion. A few morons might think I was abusing my position of authority. That's why I'd be grateful if you didn't talk about this at college – not even to Cathy.'

Lauren looks over at the bar. That girl from her English class has gone – if it was her? 'Don't worry, Grant,' she says. 'I won't tell anyone at college.'

11

And she won't, except Cathy, of course. 'I just hadn't realised you were taking such a risk.'

'You're worth it,' he says quietly. Then he says, 'We're all right for the David Lynch film at the National Film Theatre next week, aren't we.'

He could be setting a date for homework. His tone of voice is identical – to Lauren's irritation. But she had liked the way he said, 'You're worth it.' Besides, he is introducing her to things she wants to know about: good restaurants, arty cinemas. And the theatre. Her parents only ever took her to a couple of pantomimes. She'd love to go to a West End theatre. And the opera. She'll probably hate that but she'd just like to see what it's like. Then later on she can build on those tastes. It won't be with Grant, of course. It will be with – Jason is the name that won't stop popping into her head tonight.

'Your enthusiasm is very flattering,' says Grant, still waiting for her reply.

He's always so dry, so unemotional, Lauren thinks. But that's what's so appealing about him. And it's not as if she's going out with him. She could never fancy him. She's just seeing him. You can *see* as many people as you want, there's no commitment when you just *see* someone.

She senses his tenseness. He enjoys her company, doesn't he? Well, in a way she rather likes his.

12

But there's still something that stops her saying yes. She's not sure what.

'Thank you, Grant, for the invitation,' she begins.

'I'll pick you up at eight,' he interrupts.

She's heard this tone of voice in class too. That's when you know not to argue with him.

Lauren doesn't feel she can argue now.

'And this is Benny's Beefburgers,' Adam says. Even on a Thursday night the place is just packed with people their age. He shudders. He hates crowds; they always make him feel aggressive. Still, this is where people go. 'Do you fancy going in, Becky?'

She gazes in at a girl disinfecting the tables. It's not exactly romantic, is it? And it's far too busy for them to be able to talk properly. She'd hate to go in there. She says, 'Oh, I don't mind. If you want to.'

Adam studies her. What does she want? He decides to take a chance.

'If we go in there I should just warn you about one thing: all the assistants are failed doubleglazing salesmen and they take it as a personal insult if you ask for 'just one coke'. They always say, 'Are you sure you don't want one of our succulent, juicy, saliva-spinning beefburgers . . . ?' He pauses. She's laughing again. Either she laughs very easily or he's being amazingly funny tonight.

13

'No, we won't go in there then,' she says.

'Trouble is,' says Adam, 'I'm not sure where else there is to go.' He's sure there are other places. But he hasn't been out on a date for so long.

'Look, why don't you show me the sights of Cartford?'

'Well, that won't take long. Are you sure?'

'Yes, honestly.'

Adam instantly adopts a tour-guide voice. 'Just down here on your right is our chief tourist attraction, the fountain which you will observe has its very own grey water.'

'You know, the first time my mum came here to look at some houses, she brought back a postcard and it was of this fountain.'

'And you thought, now that looks like a happening town.'

'That's right. I went running up the stairs and started packing right away.' She links his arm. 'What's next then?'

All evening Adam's been trying to think who Becky reminds him of. And now it's come to him: the air hostess in those advertisements. The blonde, smiley one, who at the end of the advert used to say, 'I hope you'll fly with us again soon'. And she didn't only look like Becky, she had the same little laugh in her voice too. Adam used to watch that advert over and over.

'Up there,' he says, 'are all the really interesting

14

shops, most of which have closed down because they couldn't compete with the big chain stores. So we won't go and view their remains. But if you'd come here two years ago, I'd have taken you to Martin's Monster Toyshop, now *there* was a shop. All closed down now.' He's getting depressing, isn't he? Time to change gear. 'Up there, too was this curry house. It was only open at night and it was a real dive. Anyway, it was closed down when someone found out that they'd been shooting pigeons off their roof and putting them into their curries.'

'No!' cries Becky delightedly. 'Not really.'

'That's the honest truth,' says Adam. And it is, practically. He remembers Cathy telling him about it. Although the curry house wasn't in Cartford, it was somewhere close, though.

Becky proves to be a wonderful audience for all his anecdotes, as they walk on past the giant chain stores.

'And just ahead now is Cartford's shopping precinct, which in the day is manned by two security guards, one of whom lives two doors away from me.'

'You know all the right people, don't you?' says Becky. She's going to laugh again.

'It's all locked up now, of course,' says Adam. 'So you can only peer in at the wonders of Cartford's shopping precinct,' but as he steps forward, the automatic doors swish open. 'Well, usually they're locked,' says Adam. 'Do you want to go in?'

'Oh yes,' she cries, charging in ahead of him. She turns round grinning. 'Adam and Becky enter the Twilight Zone.' Then she says, 'Listen!' A music tape is playing on, regardless of the absence of people. 'That's Rod Stewart's "Rhythm of my Heart",' she says. 'They obviously think the sound will frighten off any intruders.'

They peer around them. The shops are still and dark and they have a faded, defeated air about them. Becky points at four bald dummies staring gloomily at them. There's something rather distasteful about seeing those dummies so exposed. They might at least have left them their wigs.

'Look here,' she cries. 'The window of the jewellery shop is smashed in.'

'Oh, that's always getting smashed in,' says Adam airily.

'Did you ever go out window-shopping and decide what you'd buy when you were rich?' asks Becky.

'Yeah, Mark and me would go around these car showrooms and all the motorbike shops.'

'With me it was always jewellery shops. And I had this marvellous ring, all picked out.'

'What kind of ring?'

'It was a sapphire ring.' She stops. He won't think she's dropping some really crass hint, will

16

he? 'I was going to buy it for myself. I still might.'
That sounds odd as well.

Luckily Adam changes the subject. 'And here,
bang in the middle of all those shops, is a café.

'With all the tables and chairs set out most invit-
ingly,' says Becky. 'I really think we are expected.'

Adam walks over to a table. 'Care to join me at
the Café New York?'

'It's not called the Café New York.'

'It is.' He points to a sign. Don't ask me why. Jez
asked this girl behind the cash till why it couldn't be
called Café Red Square instead. The girl got, well,
confused.' He moves a chair for her. Then he calls
into the silence. 'Waiter! Waiter! Sorry, the service
here is appalling.'

'I'd like to see your face if someone did appear,'
cries Becky. 'Perhaps one of those bald dummies.'

Adam stares around him, thinking how weird
this is, sitting in a café in a deserted shopping
precinct with a music tape whining over ahead and
this beautiful girl sitting opposite him. He supposes
most girls wouldn't be too impressed at ending a
date here. But Becky makes it seem a laugh, quite
exciting, in fact. She's amazing.

'There aren't any menus,' he says. 'But a pot of
tea is seventy p, a pot of coffee eighty p and sandwiches are two pounds.'

'Oh, it's quite expensive, isn't it? Still, what the

hell, I'll have the lot.' They sit back and Adam starts undoing his tie.

'I'm not used to this,' he says.

Smart clothes suit him, thinks Becky. Perhaps a little blue shirt rather than a white one, though.

'It was Mark's idea I wear a tie. This whole date was Mark's idea,' he adds. And still feels bad about that. He'll have to make it up to Mark somehow. And he must make sure Mark doesn't feel out of it.

'I owe Mark a lot,' says Becky. 'I couldn't imagine these last weeks without him.' And as she says this she can almost see Mark staring at them with that hopeful, dimpled grin of his. He's been a great friend. 'You and Mark have stayed good friends for a long time, haven't you?'

'Centuries,' says Adam. 'How about you. Have you got many good friends?'

'Well, you know what it's like. At school there'd be girls who were my closest friends and the next week they were someone else's best friend and telling everyone all my secrets, which of course were just so amazingly juicy. But with you and Mark it's different, you look out for each other. Oh yeah, what's this secret hut Mark goes on about?'

'Ah.' Adam leans forward. 'That was our secret hiding place against our enemies, who were just waiting to beat us up.' He was about to tell her how Mark had got beaten up but then thought

18

Mark might not want her to know about that. So instead he says, 'For a while it got really bad. It seemed like just about everyone in our village was against the six of us. Jason used to say it was us against the world. But the one place we were safe was in our old hut.'

'I'd love to see it. I mean, I'll let you blindfold me first and turn me round three times. Did you sign a pact in blood?'

'Not in blood,' says Adam, 'but we did sign a pact, swearing to stay friends forever.'

'Friends forever,' Becky repeats the phrase. 'It's a lovely idea. Kate was my best friend before I came here. And I've gone back a couple of times to stay with her since. We had a laugh and went to a few parties, but I don't know, it wasn't quite the same, somehow. I felt a bit out of it the last time I went down. SOB. SOB. When I met people from school I felt I was just making conversation with them, not really talking to them anymore — you know.'

'Yeah, I feel like that when I meet people in town I knew from school. In a few months' time we'll probably just nod at each other and then probably not even that. But they were never really friends, I only ever knew them on the surface.'

Most of the boys Becky's been out with only knew her on the surface. It was little more than a game really. It was nice to have a boy by your side

– sometimes. But it wasn't serious. It didn't mean anything. He didn't really care about her. And she'd pretend she didn't care. She'd tell her friends, 'I want to go out with a boy until he wants to go out with me. But I can't cope with it when he likes me.'

How her mum laughed when she said that. But this was all a clever camouflage. For really she was a shameless romantic, endlessly dreaming of a boy who would love and care for her. In her diary she'd even written once, 'I dream of a love that will grow from a tiny seed to a great bush that is always in flower.' Then underneath she'd written, 'Ugh – where's the sick bucket.' Just in case anyone ever found her diary and read that. This was her secret to be guarded fiercely at all times. Until that first day at college when she'd noticed this boy with the deepest, warmest eyes she'd ever seen . . .

'Your mum writes books, doesn't she?' asks Adam.

'Yeah. She scribbled away for years at the kitchen table, gathering all these rejections. Then the week Dad told her he was leaving us for his secretary, she got this letter inviting her in for a talk about her book, and it all happened from there. Mum's got this shed she writes in now. She's just had an advance for this new book too, which means we've got money for the first time in ages.'

'Do you read your mum's books?'

20

'Yeah. They're quite sexy for my mum.'

'I must read one.'

'I'll get her to give you a copy, signed, of course. Oh yes, that's what I meant to tell you. I think my mum's met your mum.'

Adam feels his throat suddenly very dry. 'How's that?'

'Well, my mum's doing a book-signing at The Book House next month, and last week she went there to meet the manageress and the two assistants, one of whom was called Mrs Rosen. That is your Mum, isn't it?'

Adam can only nod his head.

'My mum said she was really nice. So next time she goes in she can tell her . . . Are you all right, Adam?'

'Yes, fine,' he gasps. Then he attempts to recover himself. 'It's just these sandwiches are, stale.' But the spell is broken, and they leave a few minutes later.

Adam hails a taxi. Becky gets in the back, then starts shuffling across the car, assuming Adam will push in after her. But then she sees Adam open the door on the other side. This is what the well-mannered boy does, of course. She's just not used to such politeness. So she shuffles back again, giggling. Then Adam laughs too. And for a moment everything's easy and relaxed, just like before. But then she senses him pulling further away from her again. What's happened? What did she do wrong?

The taxi pulls up outside her house and Adam insists on paying. Then their faces lean forward and she thinks, this is it, our first kiss, something I'll always remember. But, in fact, it's deeply disappointing, with about as much passion as the ones her Great-Uncle Wilfred gives out on Christmas Day.

Adam's not so much distant now as practically disappearing over the horizon. There doesn't seem any way she can bring him back.

Grant and Lauren are sitting in his car, just down the road from Lauren's house. Outside, it's bucketing down again. 'I think I will make a dash for it,' says Lauren.

'No, you won't,' replies Grant firmly, 'as you'll only get pneumonia.'

Lauren laughs but doesn't move. Instead, she watches people scuttling past beneath umbrellas. Then suddenly Lauren notices Jez, moving surprisingly quickly for him. Where's he off to at this time? She'd have called out except she doesn't think Grant would have appreciated it. Even though Jez doesn't go to college he knows lots of people who do.

Then about two minutes later she sees him

again, running back the way he'd come. Had he gone to her house? But it's after midnight.

She peers outside. 'It's easing off now. I'd better go.' He leans forward. If he tries to kiss her, Lauren decides she won't go out with him again. But he doesn't. He just says, 'Thank you for the pleasure of your company.' His tone is both mocking and sincere. So that's all she is, just an escort for the evening. Lauren's relieved. Well, she can cope with that. It's nothing romantic, they're just *seeing* each other.

She waves him goodbye, then steams down the road. Her father is waiting for her. It's after midnight, so there's another fine. Her dad actually hands her a note, saying she owes fifty pounds. 'But I'm not that late.' she pleads. 'Couldn't you let me off this time?' And then on the hall table she sees a letter with her name on. He hasn't written her a letter too, has he? Her father's done this before when he's very angry with her.

She tears the letter open. But it's not from her father – it's from Jason. She reads:

'Dear Lauren,
    No roses this time, just me wishing I could pluck the thorn out of your heart. A thorn which I placed there on your fifteenth birthday. And which now seems destined to remain there for all eternity.

23

The sadness in my heart is now a thicket which I can never cut down. Only you can.

These words, which I could never say to your face, I finally commit to paper. Please do not show this message to anyone or talk about it to anyone – not even me. This is our secret. But at least you know.

Only three more words – I love you.

Jason.


'Oh Jason,' whispers Lauren. How could she have doubted it. She wants to ring him now. She'll have to do something. She starts to read it again. It is just so beautiful. No, she won't ring him, she'll go round to his house now. She'll throw stones up at his window and then hug and hug him in the moonlight.

'. . . was just flung through the letterbox ten minutes ago.'

She absently tunes back into her dad. What's he moaning about now.

'What was that, father?' She beams. She's bursting with happiness now and not even her dad at his grumpiest can bring her down. She's just soaring higher and higher. This is the happiest moment of her life.

'I said, that note was just hurled through the letterbox ten minutes ago, waking your poor mother up. She came rushing down the stairs. Why couldn't your friend have waited . . .'

Suddenly Lauren remembers Jez rushing by in the rain. He delivered this message – but why? If Jason wrote it, he'd deliver it. In fact, that's the part Jason would enjoy most, dashing about at night. IF HE WROTE IT.

She falls back to earth with a jolting thud. She feels cheated, angry, defeated. She can't be bothered arguing with her father any more. Instead, she crawls upstairs and lies awake in bed, hot and angry, tears streaming down her face.

Jez wrote it, of course, with Cathy. She can see Cathy's hand all over that corny message. The sadness in my heart is now a thicket which only you can cut down – oh, please. Lauren attempts a laugh. She wouldn't be surprised if Mark and Adam were in it too. She pictures them all sitting round and Cathy asking, 'How can we help poor Lauren? She's just so in love with Jason, you know.' And then they produce this.

It's a clever forgery, she'll give them that. If she hadn't seen Jez tonight she'd have believed it completely. But then she wanted to believe it. Just think if she had run round to Jason's – she'd never have lived it down. Jason didn't send those roses either. That was Cathy and Jez too.

When she thinks of all the conversations she's had with Cathy about those roses, and all the time

25

she was sending them! Well how dare they interfere like this. HOW DARE THEY. She wants to ring Cathy up now and scream at her for an hour. Then Jez. She will, first thing in the morning.

She turns over, her head throbbing. It's half-past two. She must get some sleep. But then she sits up again. No, she won't have a go at Cathy and Jez over the phone.

She's just had a better idea.

Jez is sprawled out in his bedroom feeling mighty pleased with himself. He has just created one of the world's greatest forgeries. It had taken nearly an hour to copy this message out in black ink. (Jason only ever uses black ink). Now even Jason would think he'd written it, and wish he had!

Earlier this evening Jez really had intended confessing to Jason that he'd exaggerated – if not lied his head off – about the Lauren and Jez liaison. He thought he'd confess all after the video finished. But then, early on in the video, this guy in a black mask suddenly declared, 'And truth, Sir, is a very dangerous game'. And Jez thought, you're right there, matey. And anyway, what good is it going to do telling Jason now. Will he feel better afterwards? NO. Will Jez feel better? Definitely NO.

But Jez knew he owed Jason and Lauren something. How Jez wishes he could be there when Lauren discovers his forgery.

It'll be early morning, perhaps Lauren will still be in her nightie. But as soon as she reads the note, she'll charge upstairs, get dressed, hurtle over to Jason's house and then there'll be sickeningly happy endings all round. Later on Jez will tell them about the forgery, of course. And they'll be so grateful. When they're married and living in a de luxe house (Daddy's wedding present) they'll put up a little statue of Jez in the garden, with an inscription: Jez – the main man. It has quite a nice ring to it.

Becky stands at the top of the stairs. As usual at this time she can smell coffee. Her mum will be downstairs with an absolutely massive pot of coffee bubbling away. Mum does all her writing at night in the shed. 'There are far too many distractions in the day,' she always says.

Normally the fresh, reassuring smell of coffee just takes over the house. But today, it is quickly overpowered by a nasty, bitter scent, that overnight has soaked its way into her bones – the scent of failure. ADAM DIDN'T ASK HER OUT AGAIN.

Becky stumbles down the stairs. Never had a night lasted so long. She even convinced herself everything was going backwards when, after becoming lighter, she had slept and then woke up to find darkness again. She's still not sure what happened.

She nods at her mum, who looks up in surprise. She knows Becky hasn't got a class until half-past ten today and she is not the world's earliest riser. But before Becky can explain she hears the snap of the letterbox and rushes out into the hall. The post is early. But there's only one letter and it's not stamped and it's got her name on it. She rips it open and reads:

SPECIAL OFFER – FOR *BECKY* ONLY.
LAST NIGHT YOU SAMPLED AN EVEN-ING OUT WITH ADAM. IF YOU ARE READY, WILLING AND FOOLISH ENOUGH TO RECEIVE THESE DELIGHTS INTO YOUR LIFE ON A REG-ULAR BASIS, JUST TICK APPROPRIATE BOX AND POST THIS CARD FOR AN IMMEDIATE RESPONSE. (*Personal callers at college very welcome. c/o Science block*).
 YES (GO-ON, PLEASE INVITE ME)
 NO WAY.
P.S. *Last night was the best of my life.*
*Adam* XXXXXXXXXXX

The third time she stares at it, it's as if the words can't contain their excitement any longer. They've got to get up and do something. And so has she. She bursts into the kitchen where her mum is still hunched over a mug of coffee, calls out, 'Won't be a minute, Mum,' and before her mum has even looked up Becky's leaped out of the house and down the road.

It's been raining most of the night and cars stream past, gushing spray all over the pavement. But Becky doesn't care about any of that. She's just wishing she was a bit more fit as she rushes to catch Adam up. She turns into Merton Close, panting like crazy now. If any of her friends saw her they wouldn't believe it. Becky makes a point of never running – not for a bus, not for anything. And then she sees him, right at the end of Merton Close.

'Adam,' she cries. Please turn round. Don't make me run down the road towards you, as I look really awful when I run. I know I do.

A school bus stops and there's an almighty scrum of school children, plus a conductor, screeching, 'Form a queue, form a queue!' Adam can't hear her over that racket. She practically screams his name now, 'Adam.' This time he turns round immediately. And then he stares at her, like he can't believe she's there, before tearing up the road to her. And the sight of him rushing towards her is something she will never forget, not even when she's a little old lady mumbling to herself in a home. She'll forget other things, but never that. He's run so fast he's too out of breath to speak at first. Then she gasps something about the letter and all at once his arms are around her and he's lost in her warmth. She brushes her lips against his cheek and then he kisses her gently on the lips. And her lips taste slightly salty. They remind Adam of the sea. Now they kiss again. Only this time the kiss just flows on and on. Several planets away he can dimly hear voices around them, laughing and commenting. But much louder is a strange roaring in his head, like the sea. It is the sea and he's riding a giant wave which is lifting him higher and higher. Even after the kiss ends her body's still pressing tightly against his.

'I wanted so badly to ask you out last night,' he says.

'So why didn't you?' Her voice is light, almost teasing.

'My mum thinks I should only go out with Jewish girls. I thought she might give you grief . . . I didn't think I could ask you to take that on. It didn't seem fair.'

'Was that all?'

Adam stares at her, in disbelief. Last night it had seemed an impossible obstacle.

He kisses her hair. 'You really don't mind?'

'No, besides, I'll win her round,' says Becky. 'Mothers like me.'

'But we'll pick our moment,' says Adam. 'For now . . .'

'For now it's our secret,' interrupts Becky.

Across the road he sees his bus come and go. But there'll be other buses. He can't go, not yet. Instead, he stands watching her disappear up Merton Close. The way her hair bounces behind her, as if it had a life force all of its own. She's incredible and now she's mine.

To think he nearly didn't ask her out because of his parents. They'll rant on a bit at first. But in the end they'll see what's important. What could be more important than the fact that Adam's heart, which he thought had stopped for good, is now beating faster than ever.

# 2 Playing the Truth Game

'You can take the crown jewels out of your ears now.' Mr Fanshaw, the manager of Radleys Supermarket, is glaring down at Cathy. He is having a surprise inspection just before opening time. Cathy pulls off the earrings. This is like being at school again. She'd only worn those earrings, a birthday present from Lauren, to cheer herself up after yet another nasty breakfast encounter with Giles.

'She's wearing nail polish too, she's been told about his before, hasn't she, Mr Lurie?'

Mr Lurie, the deputy manager, is doing his impression of an empty suit of clothes – and most successfully, too. But Mr Fanshaw is able to answer his own questions. 'Yes, you have, young lady,' he declares, waving a podgy finger alarmingly near Cathy's nose. 'We don't mind you wearing make-up, provided it's subtle, but it must be SUBTLE!

Cathy thinks he's the most unsubtle-looking man she's ever seen. He's got a bashed-in nose, no right ear – lost, according to Radleys gossip, in a knife fight – and hasn't bothered getting a neck either. Why bother, when he has such a huge jaw and positively mountainous shoulders. His eyes bulge so alarmingly, you wouldn't be surprised if one of them popped out of its socket. He really is a monster and Cathy's only consolation is that his face is such a fierce, unhealthy red that he surely can't live much longer.

Mr Fanshaw moves his tour of inspection on to Jez, looking, as usual, as if he's just spent the night crashed out on someone's floor after an epic party. Yesterday Jez had to go and see Mr Fanshaw, or Baked Bean Man as Jez calls him, for his second warning.

This morning Baked Bean Man's eyes linger unlovingly on Jez's.

'Don't forget to get your hair cut like I said, he snarls. 'And wear black trousers not black jeans. Got it?'

'Certainly, mon Capitaine,' says Jez, his eyes glinting with bleary amusement.

Baked Bean Man's eyes are arctic. 'I'm watching you,' he mutters. Then his large, wet lips attempt a bit of stretching. 'I am here to praise as well,' he declares. He is standing in front of Stephen, who was in Cathy's year at school, but is now working here full-time.

'Right away I noticed your work. I said to Mr Lurie, now that's a well-stocked shelf . . .'

'Oooh, what a lovely shelf,' hisses Jez.

'And now you are working on the till. Is that right?'

'Yes, I am, Sir, thank you, Sir.'

'Clean your underpants for you, Sir,' whispers Jez.

'Don't,' says Cathy. Any second now she'll burst out laughing. She does that sometimes. And she can't think of a worse time for it to happen than now. Yet, although it's funny, it's also somehow rather shocking to see a boy from her year at school enter so quickly into the mentality of this place. As Jez said, 'He's a company man already'.

Cathy sometimes had lunch here and recently she was sitting talking to Stephen when he pointed over at the hallowed table, where only those in charge of tills are permitted to sit, and said, 'Their table is always cleaner than ours, did you notice that?'

And actually Cathy had, but only in passing. It was like this was his ambition now, to sit at a clean table with the till supervisors.

Baked Bean Man walks down the line now to the older workers and if none of them actually curtsey they certainly come pretty close. Then he

34

says, 'Over the next week there may well be other checks, because one week from today, our chairman, Mr Christie, is paying us an official visit. This is a great honour for us.' Various staff act like bit-part actors and murmur their agreement. 'And it is vital that he sees us at our best. He waves his fist right in the air, 'And nothing must *go wrong*. Everything must be right.' He pauses before punching out the last word, 'PERFECT.'

Jez winks at Cathy. For he alone here knows the surprise Cathy has planned for that day – a big demonstration outside the supermarket against meat eating. Over the past few days she's thought of nothing else. And now she's feeling distinctly scared. For Baked Bean Man is a thug, isn't he? And her natural instincts tell her not to cross thugs. But then she remembers what happened last night . . . A piece of meat had come through unpriced and she had to take it out the back to the meat room. She tried not to think about what she was doing and just strode through the plastic doors. But the first thing she saw was this man cutting up a pig. He had blood splashed all over his white apron and there were even splodges of blood on his white wellies. And the whole place reeked of blood that had gone off a bit – a vile, fishy smell. There was no way Cathy could stay in there and in the end she had to wait outside, tightly holding her nose while the butcher priced the meat up. For

35

the rest of that shift she couldn't stop trembling. It was just so barbaric, so cruel. And surely no civilised person could go on eating meat after spending five minutes in there. People hide their faces away from what's going on. Well, next week she's going to make them see. She's got to, no matter what the consequences. What are a few moments of aggro compared with saving animals lives?

The inspection of his troops completed, Baked Bean Man marches back to his office 'to watch us on the small screen', as Jez puts it.

The staff gather in small clusters for a quick gossip before the doors open. Cathy notices how Stephen is standing quite away from her and Jez, as if they're a bad influence.

Jez yawns.

'Jez, you look even worse than usual.'

'I'm out of it,' he yawns. 'Only had a wash ten minutes ago. But I'm looking forward to Baked Bean Man bursting a few blood vessels next Thursday. How many people have you got for your demo?'

'About a hundred so far,' whispers Cathy. 'And right now I'm feeling really nervous about it. By the way, Lauren's invited herself and me round your house tonight.'

'I'll probably be dead on the floor somewhere, but fine.'

'It was going to be round my house but the atmosphere between Giles and me is just so poisonous at the moment . . .'

'No, that's all right. My humble home is at your disposal.'

'She rang me up first thing this morning, just in case she missed me at college. She sounded rather strange so I said, "There's nothing wrong, is there?" And she goes, "Oh, no," and then I asked about Grant and she said hardly anything really. She was definitely funny, somehow. Why are you smiling?'

'Well, I think Lauren will have some news for us tonight.'

'What kind of news?'

'Oh, good news,' says Jez, grinning. 'Very good news. You'll be delighted. Anyway, I'd better go and scare a few customers.'

'Hold up, Jez, what good news?' cries Cathy. 'You can't leave me like this.'

'Yes, I can,' laughs Jez. 'I mean, it's only a hunch, mind, but I think you're going to be pretty happy tonight.'

'Hi Mark, it's only me,' Becky's voice crackles down the phone. She sounds as if she's just been running but then she always sounds a bit like that. 'I just rang up to say everything went really well last night and we owe it all to you.'

Mark can't help feeling chuffed. 'I thought that restaurant would be a good one and I got you the table all the couples want.'

'Fancy meeting up before History?' She laughs slightly. 'Then I can tell you all the gory details.'

Actually, Becky doesn't need to tell Mark anything. Just one look at Becky tells it all. Even her hair positively shines. Young love, thinks Mark, feeling at least forty-five.

Then at lunchtime Cathy comes rushing back from Radleys to hear all about it. And all the time Becky is enthusing about Adam, Mark notices that Cathy keeps sneaking these little glances at him. So his smile grows more and more fixed, until he feels as if he has a coat-hanger in his mouth. But the last thing he wants is sympathy.

He's looking forward to the end of the day when he and Becky go off to the café they wryly call 'our café'. It is so untrendy, hardly any other students go there. It means, though, you haven't got to be worried about being overheard. And Becky's always particularly relaxed there.

Yet today, who should they see wating outside college for them but Adam. The science block, where Adam is based, is about a mile away and the classes tend to go on longer than theirs, so Mark doesn't usually see Adam then. But today, there he is, saying, 'I had an urgent dental appointment today, the first of many,' and then he and Becky are kissing, really kissing.

In the past, he and Adam had passed couples kissing passionately by the school gates. And they'd watched them curiously and more than a bit enviously. It made Mark always feel suddenly immature and uninformed somehow. He feels that now, only more so.

And this kissing goes on and on, while Mark wonders if he should walk on and leave them. But they might think he'd gone off in a mood. And he certainly doesn't want them thinking that. So in the end he calls out, 'Don't you think you'd better come up for air now,' just so they'd know he's still there.

Then they both start laughing and all three are walking to 'our café (which Mark is already re-christening 'their café'). Mark can't help noticing the way Adam's hand just curls around Becky so easily, so naturally. Isn't it strange how life changes. Less than twenty-four hours ago Mark was the go-between, the vital link between Adam and Becky and the architect of their first date. Now, overnight, he's been made redundant. Suddenly Becky grabs his hand and they're both beaming practically identical smiles on him. Mark knows their thoughts are identical too: poor old Mark, mustn't let him feel out of it. That's when Mark knows it's time for him to exit fast.

He stops outside the sports shop where Jason works. 'I'm going to see if my trainers are in,' he says. 'You two go on.'

'No, we'll wait,' say Becky and Adam. Already they're talking in chorus.

'No, that's all right. I want to talk to Jason about something confidential,' says Mark.

Adam's looking distinctly hurt now, so Mark adds, 'I'll catch you up, won't be long.'

Inside, a tired-looking guy in a pale blue track suit speeds up to Mark, then, recognising him as one of Jason's mates, gives a faint smile and disappears again. Jason is in the back of the shop with a large pasty-faced boy and an even larger pasty-looking woman, who can only be his mother. The mother is staring anxiously at her son as he pounds up and down in his new trainers.

'Only get them if you want, Wilfred. We can always try the other sports shop,' she adds, in a piercing whisper.

'I don't know if these are best or not,' wails Wilfred.

In a low voice, Jason says, 'My training partner always wears those.' Wilfred and his mum both stare at Jason.

'You go out running then?' asks Wilfred's mother.

'Every morning, just for an hour or two,' says Jason.

Mark suppresses a laugh. Running is one sport – well, Jason won't even call it a sport – that he hates. And he got a Saturday morning detention for skiving off cross-country.

Jason rolls his eyes, 'I'm saving up for a pair myself.'

'I'll take them,' cries the boy, waving the trainers at Jason.

'And if you have any problems, just ask for Jason. May I give you one of my cards.'

After they leave, Mark claps his hands.

'Psychology, that's what it's all about,' says Jason. But they're good trainers even though he'll have grown out of them in a few months. On your own today then, Markie?'

'Yeah, Adam and Becky invited me to go off with them for coffee but I thought they'd prefer to be on their own.'

'Last night went off all right, then?'

'Yeah.'

'I bet they're grateful to you.'

Mark doesn't answer.

'So, Markie, how's college. Met any fast women?'

'Yeah, loads, only they're so fast I don't get to see them.'

Jason laughs. 'Never mind mate, your time's

coming. Oh yeah, your trainers are in, hold up a sec.'

By the time Jason returns from the stockroom Mark is already sitting down and pulling off his old trainers. Only, in haste, he pulls off his right sock as well. 'Hey, Jason, I've got five white hairs on this ankle, look.' He's oddly proud of these white hairs. 'And I've got a couple on my left ankle. Want to see?'

'No, couldn't stand the excitement,' says Jason. He watches Mark pace up and down the shop.

'What do you think of them?' asks Mark.

'You look the business now mate,' says Jason.

'Really?' Mark flushes with pleasure. 'How much did you say these were?'

'Well, they are seventy pounds but I put you down for a staff discount, so they're forty pounds to you. Last pair in the shop,' adds Jason. 'We can't keep up with the demand.'

'I'll have the money next week,' says Mark. 'Can you keep 'em here for me until then?'

Jason considers for a second. 'Take 'em now,' he says suddenly.

'Are you sure?' Mark's face is one big smile now.

'Yeah, you've got an honest face and the boss is away for a week. Left me in charge of course . . .'

'What's it like being in charge then?' asks Mark.

'I love it,' confesses Jason. 'And I've got plans for this place. You see, you've got to put yourself

42

in the customer's place. Make them welcome, greet them but don't jump on them.' The phone rings. 'Won't be a sec,' says Jason. Then Mark hears him say, 'Good afternoon, Warner Sports and Leisure Shop, Jason Kent speaking, how may I help you?'

Mark shakes his head in admiration. Everything Jason does, he does with such style, such class. Some people say he's a big-head. Well maybe he is but then Jason's got lots to be big-headed about. Yet he looks out for his mates too. And he can be so funny sometimes. There's really no one like him. Sometimes Mark thinks if he could be anyone in the world, it would be Jason.

He prowls around the sports shop. He feels lighter and more agile already. No girl could fail to notice him gliding about in these trainers. In fact, he wouldn't be surprised if these trainers changed his life. He watches the guy in the pale blue track suit trying to sell some trainers to a family. But he hasn't got Jason's expertise. And then he sees Clive Sturgess enter the sports shop.

Clive is in their English group and has been sniffing around Becky since the beginning of term. There aren't many boys in the English group and Clive obviously thinks he's the main male attraction. He's also one of these people who thinks he's really witty. And whenever you talk to him you can tell he's not really listening to you, just trying to think of the next funny line. When he's not being funny he's smirking. And Mark has noticed that whatever he says Sturgess immediately starts smirking, as if Mark is just one big joke.

'No harem today then?'

Usually when Clive sees Mark he's with Becky, and sometimes Cathy and Lauren too. Mark doesn't answer him.

'On your own today then?'

Mark looks up at him. How can Becky think he's got nicely shaped eyes. He nearly threw up when she said that. And Sturgess is wearing one of those striped shirts that Mark used to wear when he was three years old.

'No, I'm here with twenty other people,' says Mark.

'I didn't know you knew twenty people, Mark,' says Sturgess. Smirk Smirk. 'No Becky, then,' he adds.

'No, she's off with her boyfriend.'

Clive's mouth does a bit of twisting now. 'Since when?'

'Why?' asks Mark. 'What's it to you?'

'I thought you were her boyfriend.'

But Mark knows Clive never thought that. He turns away; let him go and slime off somewhere else. He starts walking towards Jason. He's still on the phone. Mark eavesdrops.

'May I take your name? Denise Pine. You wouldn't believe me if I said Denise was one of

44

my favourite names, would you.' He laughs. Mark can almost hear the girl laughing too. 'You sound like you're very attractive. You are. Well, that's one thing we've got in common.'

'Heard about Lauren?'

Mark whirls round. Clive Sturgess is breathing down on to his hair.

'What about her?'

'She's knocking off Grantie.'

'No, I don't think so,' says Mark. But strangely enough, he remembers Becky asking him about Lauren and Grant after lunch. She said there was a rumour going round college that Lauren was going out with him. But he'd been so preoccupied with other things that he'd forgotten all about it.

'No, I've heard from a very good source that Grantie is knocking her off. So she won't have to worry about her English.' Clive doesn't say any more. He can't. Jason's hand is wrapped tightly round his throat.

Mark stands back stunned. No arrow could have reached its target more swiftly than Jason moved. And he hadn't even realised Jason was listening to their conversation.

'I don't even want to hear her name on your lips again. Right?' says Jason.

Mark's heard those words in a film, probably one he watched with Jason. But Jason means it all right. Clive Sturgess makes what sounds like

45

agreeing noises but it's difficult to tell. Jason relaxes his hold; his hand is just leaning against Sturgess's throat now. 'Get out of my shop now,' he hisses.

Sturgess positively gallops to the door but before leaving he cries, 'You ought to be locked up.'

The family being served by the guy in the pale blue track suit make a very hasty exit, too.

'I nearly had a sale there,' he wails. 'What was that all about?' Jason doesn't say anything for a moment and his eyes have a strange, empty look in them. Mark's seen that look in his face before, just after he's struck someone.

'I didn't like the colour of his shirt,' he says. 'It didn't go with his eyes.' Then he half whispers to Mark, 'What he said about Lauren . . .'

'First I've heard about it.'

'Who is this Grant?'

'He's an English lecturer.'

'Old?'

'Oh, yeah,' says Mark. 'Well, pretty old, thirtyish.'

'Lauren . . . she . . . she . . .' Then he shakes his head and picks up the phone again. 'Sorry about that,' he says.

Mark still can't believe what he saw. The way Jason just sprang at him like that. Wham. Amazing. And while he was chatting up another girl, too. He wishes Lauren could have seen that.

He stands staring out of the window, wondering

if Sturgess would come back with some mates to get his revenge. But no, that's not really Sturgess's style. It's then he sees Adam and Becky walking back down from 'our café'. They've come to pick him up, haven't they? They're trying so hard not to let him feel out of things. But it's useless. It's as if they're inside a beautiful, de luxe house with a log fire blazing away in the corner, gazing out at Mark, stuck in a cold, damp, dreary day like this one. And they wave and smile at Mark but all they're doing is making him feel colder. Much colder.

A hand pats him on the shoulder. It's Jason. He doesn't say anything for a moment. Then as Adam and Becky walk into the shop, Jason whispers, 'Life's a bitch.'

'I know what we can do,' declares Lauren suddenly. 'We can play a game of truth.'

'What do we want to play that for?' asks Jez, still a little peeved that she and Cathy had rejected the horror videos he'd hired for this evening.

Cathy and Lauren are sitting on the settee and Jez is sprawled across the carpet.

'We haven't played that for years,' says Cathy. 'Not since that time we were in British Home Stores.'

'I remember,' says Jez. 'We all had to say what

each other's good and bad points were. And you walked out, Lauren.'

'I didn't.'

'You did, Lauren,' says Cathy. 'It was when we all said you were spoilt.'

'Oh, well, you all ganged up on me.'

'And we thought you'd just gone for a joke, at first,' says Jez, 'so we all sat there thinking, Lauren'll come back in a minute. But you'd gone home and when we rang you up you were in such a sulk.' He starts laughing.

'Oh, that was years and years ago,' says Lauren, briskly. 'And there were too many of us playing then, three's just right.'

'You're really keen to play this, aren't you?' says Cathy. 'I wonder why. Usually people use the truth game when there is something they want to bring out into the open.'

Jez leans forward. 'Is there something you want to tell us, Lauren, because we're your friends and you can tell us anything.'

'I'm not saying – yet,' says Lauren.

'I think there is,' says Jez. 'All evening you've been looking at us from under your eyelids.'

'I haven't.'

'Oh, yes, you have. What are you up to, Lauren?'

'Nothing. I just feel like a game of truth, that's all.'

Jez shakes his head. Who ever feels like a game

of truth. She's definitely up to something. Is it to do with that letter from Jason. Why hasn't she said anything about it when he thought that would have been the first thing she'd have mentioned.

'But this time,' adds Lauren, 'we're going to play it properly. Go and get some paper and pens, Jez.'

'Oh, what?' moans Jez. 'This is all getting very serious. Do we really want to do this?'

'Yes, we do, don't we Cathy?' says Lauren.

'Definitely,' says Cathy. 'I want to know what you're up to.'

'Oh, Jez,' Lauren calls after him. 'Get a jam jar or something, too.'

Jez goes into the kitchen where his mum and dad are sitting at the table staring at a little black and white television. As soon as Jez walks in his mum jumps up. 'Want some tea?' she asks.

'No, writing paper,' he grins. 'Can I take a few sheets off here?' He picks up the notepad on which Mum writes little reminders to herself.

'I've got some nicer writing paper upstairs. Let me get that,' she says.

'No, this is fine, Mum.'

'Are you sure?' When Jez's mum knew Lauren was coming round she leapt around the lounge trying to push the curtains together (somehow they never quite met), straightening and dusting all the little ornaments and depositing these white, crinkly serviettes everywhere. And then after she'd finished, she sank back on the settee and declared, wearily, 'Unlike Lauren's mother, I've never had the house I wanted, you know. I've always had to compromise.'

If, at that moment, someone had dropped and envelope containing a thousand pounds into Jez's hand, he'd have certainly handed it all to his mum.

'I'll take some pens as well, Mum,' says Jez. 'Oh, yeah, and have you got a jam jar?'

His mum is immediately on her knees searching through the cupboard.

'Got a pickle jar?'

'That's great,' says Jez.

'Having a quiz are you, son?' asks his dad, his eyes still firmly fixed on the screen.

'Something like that, Dad,' replies Jez.

Back in the lounge Lauren is getting impatient. 'Come on, pass the paper and pens out, Jez,' she says.

'I feel like I'm about to do an exam,' says Jez, dropping down on the carpet again.

'Now we write our name first, don't we?' says Cathy. 'Then the name of the person we want to ask a question, and then the question.'

'And if you think someone's lying you shout liar,' adds Lauren.

'Only you never really know if someone's lying, do you?' says Jez.

'I know when you're lying,' says Cathy.

50

'How?'

'I don't know. I just do.'

'Right, I've finished my question,' says Lauren.

Jez watches her curiously. She seemed to know exactly what she wanted to ask. And now her left foot is tapping impatiently, as if she can't wait for them to finish. What is going on?

Now Cathy's turning to her and smiling. Is that a conspiratorial smile? Are they both up to something? Jez has a feeling he's going to regret playing this game.

'This is silly,' mutters Jez as he folds his question over and puts it into the jar.

'Shall we let Cathy shake them up and pick one out,' says Lauren.

Jez nods.

'All right, here goes,' says Cathy, reaching into the jar.

Oh, one rule you didn't mention, Lauren. If someone refuses to answer a question they say, I don't want to answer that question on the grounds that ... and then they give their reason. And it's up to us to say if we accept it or not.' She shivers. 'This is getting quite good, isn't it?'

'Just get on with it, Cathy,' says Jez.

'ALL RIGHT. The first question is from ...' She unfolds the paper, 'Oh, how embarrassing – it's from me.'

'Fix,' says Jez.

'And my question is for Jez.'

'I knew it would be me,' says Jez. 'I just knew it.'

'Jez, my question is: when you came back after being away for over a year, how did you think Lauren and I had changed?'

'I don't want to answer that question,' says Jez at once.

'On what grounds?' asks Cathy.

'On the grounds that it's a pathetic question. Is that the best you can do, Cathy?'

'Not accepted,' says Lauren. 'It's a good question and you've got to answer it.'

'But I can't answer a moronic question like that,' says Jez.

'Why's it moronic?' asks Cathy indignantly.

'Go on, Jez, answer it,' says Lauren.

'All right, let me think for a moment. All right, serious now . . . Cathy, in the year that I was away you . . . er . . . blossomed.'

'Blossomed,' echoes Lauren, doubtfully. 'That's not the right word.'

'Look, who's doing this?' says Jez. 'And Lauren, you've blossomed too. You've both now blossomed into wonderful, beautiful . . .'

'I think he should do a forfeit for grovelling,' says Cathy.

'I notice neither of you called out liar, though,' says Jez.

'Let's have another go, Cathy,' says Lauren.

'Dig deep this time,' says Jez.

'And this question is from Lauren,' says Cathy,' and it's for Jez.'

'Oh, what a surprise,' says Jez. 'You two have planned this. You're stitching me up, aren't you?'

'Not at all,' says Cathy, 'and Lauren's question is . . .' She pauses, 'What a funny question. She asks: why did you go to my house at a quarter to one this morning?'

Jez starts violently. 'I will not answer that question,' he says immediately.

'On what grounds,' snaps Lauren.

'On the grounds I don't know what you're talking about.'

'I saw you.' There's no mistaking the harshness in her voice now. Jez can feel himself shrivelling up. 'Oh, that wasn't me,' he says. 'There's this guy who's always getting mistaken for me,' he laughs desperately. 'We're practically identical twins.'

'It was you,' repeats Lauren, glaring at him. 'And he delivered something – didn't he Cathy?'

Cathy, who's been shifting her gaze from one to the other, looks at Lauren, eyes wide and startled. 'ME, I don't know anything about this.'

'I think you do,' says Lauren. 'I think you helped Jez write this.'

She pulls out of her bag the note from Jason and thrusts it in front of Cathy.

'But this is from Jason,' gasps Cathy.

'No, it bloody isn't,' says Lauren, her voice rising. 'It's a pathetic forgery which you, my best friend, helped to write.'

'I never did,' cries Cathy.

'Liar! Liar! Liar!' shrieks Lauren.

'Hold up, Lauren you'll have my mum in here,' says Jez.

'Good. Let them know what deceitful friends I've got. How could you?'

'Lauren, please believe me,' cries Cathy, reaching out and touching Lauren's arm, 'I never wrote this. I swear to you on my life.'

At this, Lauren crumples a little. 'And do you swear too Jez – on your life?'

'Not on my life, no, but I'll swear on someone else's'. He pulls at the carpet. On an ordinary day the carpet's reds and blacks and blues are pretty loud – today they're positively screeching. 'Lauren, I wrote that silly message from Jason and it was, as they say, all my own work. I'll swear on my own life about that.'

'But why?' gasps Cathy.

Jez gets up. 'I can't talk with you both giving me daggers. I feel as if I'm on trial.' He leaves a gap for a friendly smile or word but none come. They're both just sitting there eyeballing him. Even the carpet's easier to look at than them.

'My identical twin did it and I'd like to tell you why.' He paces the room, staring up at the ceiling.

'Once upon a time this guy, we'll call him J – so you can't guess who he is – met a beautiful young damsel called L, and every time he gazed upon this damsel, lust permeated his soul. One fine day L and J went out boogieing and there was rejoicing in the land after that. But next day L was out boogieing with another guy, and another guy the next day. It was then J realised that when L gazed upon his manly features, lust didn't so much as graze her soul, and he was very sad.' He pauses, gazing now at he ornaments on the mantelpiece, their blank stares oddly soothing.

'But then L went out with one of J's best mates – we'll call him the Prince. And old J was as jealous as could be. Then one night the did something nasty, a real Julius Caesar back-stab. He told the Prince lies about L.'

'What kind of lies?' asks Lauren, speaking more quickly now than before.

'Wicked J pretended he and L had gone out together until one day she just dumps him. This story really gutted the Prince – and the very next day the Prince and L broke up – at L's party, as a matter of fact. Ever since, J has had to push what happened to the back of his mind, but the guilt just wouldn't go away. In fact, it grew. That's why last night he composed that silly note and pushed it through your door and now – now he's going to die, isn't he?' He finally dares to look at Lauren.

'Well, say something, have a wobbly, stick your stillettos up my trousers, haul me on to the carpet for a good whipping . . .'

But she doesn't say anything. She's just sitting staring at him. And so's Cathy, their faces locked into one incredulous expression. It's like staring at two more ornaments.

He laughs nervously. 'I told you I didn't like the game . . . What else can I say, Lauren, but I'm sorry, really, truly, gut-wrenchingly sorry.'

Lauren can remember him saying the same words to her, it was years ago. Just after her birthday, in fact. He was playing with this pet rabbit her father had bought her – really expensive, too – when it got away from him. And they never found it. That's when he said those same words and gave the same nervous smile as he's giving her now. Suddenly, it feels just as if it's Jez's twelve-year-old self that is now peeping out from beneath that eyesore of a beard. That's when she gets up and does exactly what she did then: she hugs him as hard as she can. 'It's all right,' she says. 'It's not important.' He pulls away from her, half-smiling. 'Don't be nice to me, Lauren, the shock will kill me.'

She's laughing, too. 'That's what I was hoping for, actually.'

Jez starts breathing furiously. 'Air – I'd almost forgotten what breathing in felt like . . . Ha, that's better. Just for the record, Lauren, did you really see me?'

'Yes, I was in Grant's car waiting for the rain to stop when you ran past.'

He shakes his head. 'So if it hadn't started raining . . .'

'I might never have seen you and maybe I might . . . but no, it was too well-written for Jason. To be honest, I thought it was too well-written for you.'

'Oh, thanks.'

'The other notes and flowers?'

'Nothing to do with me. Honest. So they must be Jason.'

Lauren ignores this.

'Cathy, I owe you a complete apology.'

'Yes, you do,' says Cathy.

'I'll make it up to you, Cathy, I promise. I wasn't thinking straight, otherwise I'd never have thought you were in it. I'm sorry.'

Cathy doesn't reply, she just tilts her head back on the chair, as if she's getting ready to go to sleep.

'Now you know it was me,' begins Jez . . .

'Jason still shouldn't have done what he did to me,' she says firmly.

'But at least you know why,' says Jez. 'Which reminds me . . .' he rushes over to the jar, 'of my question, which is for you, Lauren, and it is . . .'

he unfolds the letter, 'and remember the same rules still apply, don't they, Cathy?'

Cathy doesn't reply but he rushes on, 'What do you, Lauren, honestly think of Jason. You've got to answer.'

'Well, I . . .'

'Come on, the truth,' says Jez.

'All right, sometimes I wish I'd never met Jason.' She pauses.

'But?' prompts Jez.

'There are no buts.'

'Liar,' cries Jez. A car horn explodes outside.

'And that's my dad. He said he was picking me up tonight to make sure I was on time,' says Lauren.

'Oh, come on ref, that's not fair, is it Cathy?' But Cathy seems to be miles away.

'We're playing this game tomorrow night,' says Jez.

'You can,' says Lauren, 'but I'm going out with Grant. But perhaps that answers your question.'

'No,' says Jez, 'it doesn't.'

Now Jez's mother is standing in the doorway. 'I think that's your father's car, Lauren, dear.'

'Yes, thanks, Mrs Stephens. Look, I must go. I'll ring you first thing tomorrow, Cathy. Thank you, Jez, for a fascinating evening.' She adds gently, 'No more letters.'

He grins sheepishly.

After she's gone Jez feels oddly embarrassed. 'Well, this had been an evening to grip the bowels. I don't know, you sit round for a nice quiet evening with your pals and then suddenly you're up to your armpits in dynamite. Still, I suppose it's cleared the air, now you know my guilty secret.' But the air isn't so much clear as eerily still.

'You're very quiet,' he says.

Cathy looks up, her face almost wooden. 'Stunned,' she says. Then she gets up.

'You're not going, are ya?'

'Yeah, lot to do tomorrow.'

'But tomorrow's Saturday.'

'I've still got to get all the posters finished for the demonstration and . . . lots of other things.'

'Well, at least have another coffee or something.'

'No, I won't, thanks.'

'What's wrong?'

'Nothing.'

'Yes, there is, you've gone all droopy.'

'Half an hour ago I was blooming,' she shrugs her shoulders. 'I'm just a bit tired, that's all.'

'All right then, Cathy, I'll see you out.'

'There's no need,' she says, stiffly polite.

'Come on, Cathy,' says Jez. 'Why are you acting all moody. It's not like you. Come on, stay, enjoy yourself and have a custard cream.'

Cathy doesn't even answer this, just walks quickly away.

59

# 3 Cathy and Jason in Big Trouble

'It doesn't make me look fat, does it?' Cathy turns round questioningly to Becky.

'Not at all. I'd say it's figure-hugging,' says Becky.

'And you think I should buy it?'

'Oh, yes, definitely.'

Cathy's already tried the blue dress twice, the second time with Lauren in attendance, urging her to buy it. But Cathy still wasn't sure. That's why she enlisted Becky's help this time. And she's still not certain.

The assistant, whom Becky had christened 'Kinky boots', hovers, 'How are we getting on?' she asks, with more than a trace of weariness.

'I think I'll buy it,' says Cathy. 'But I need to think it over tonight. Sorry,' she adds guiltily.

'At least put a deposit down on it,' says Becky,

and she's already whipping out her cheque book. 'I'll pay the deposit for you as my dad's just sent me another cheque.

'No, that's all right. I can pay,' says Cathy at once.

Outside, Cathy says, 'Thanks again for looking at the dress with me. I just wish I was more impulsive.'

'I wish I was a bit less impulsive,' replies Becky. 'I just look at a dress and think, yes. Then afterwards, I spend hours wondering why on earth I bought it. Coffee?' she adds.

'Yeah, great.' Cathy looks at her watch. 'I'm supposed to be meeting Jason in a few minutes. He's going to try and get a local paper to come to the demo tomorrow. So I'll just pop up the road and tell him where we're going. Where are we going, by the way?'

'To the most exclusive café in town,' grins Becky.

As they enter the café, Becky says, 'Mark and I come here most days. We have a kind of warped affection for it. But Adam only came here the once and absolutely hated it. So don't worry if you hate it too.'

It is, as usual, practically empty apart from a couple of women hissing gossip in the corner, a man in a suit stuffing chips into his mouth and an old woman in a grey coat and pale blue trousers, cuddling her empty cup.

'Charming hole, isn't it?' says Becky.

They order a pot of coffee for two and sit gossiping for a few minutes. Cathy watches Becky closely. Yesterday, Lauren was saying that she thought Becky was just like a girl who used to wash their hair at Diane's hair salon a couple of years ago. This girl, Cathy thinks her name was Gail, was incredibly bubbly and smiley. And she was always really well made-up; Lauren said she must have got through a packet of foundation a day. Then one day she just wasn't there any more. She didn't give any notice, only a note saying how everything was getting her down. 'And, actually,' recalled Lauren, 'she had quite a few skeletons in her closet. And so, I bet, has Becky,' Lauren went on. 'I mean, no one smiles as much as she does: Miss Friend to everyone. It's not natural.'

'She's in love,' replied Cathy.

Lauren just laughed, cynically.

She smiles coyly at Becky. 'And how's Adam?'

Becky gives an equally coy smile. 'Wonderful.' She pauses for a moment, then says, 'You know, he's not at all like the kind of guy I went out with before. I went out with awful blokes before. You know, the kind who stand in pubs with their legs six yards apart trying to look hard.'

'Oh, I can't stand them,' says Cathy.

'Neither can I, now,' says Becky. 'I see them strutting around at college and think, how pathetic. And they give their girl friends such a hard time. My dad used to hate them, too. I mean, if one of those guys opened a door for you or something, which was so unusual, they'd talk about it for weeks afterwards. And Adam just does those things automatically, it's part of his nature. I like that. Perhaps I wasn't ready for that before. But now, I want someone who's going to look out for me.' Becky starts stirring her coffee. 'He called me Lisa yesterday. Just the once but he was terribly embarrassed about it. What was Lisa like?'

'I think she was nice. But I didn't really know her.'

'And when she died he took it really badly, didn't he?'

'Yes. It was awful seeing him like that. You'd be talking to him and yet it was like he wasn't there.' Becky is staring intently at her now. 'I remember visiting him, must have been a couple of weeks afterwards. And he told me he wanted to dig a big hole and go and sit in the bottom of it, then things could go on and it wouldn't matter as he'd be away from them.'

'I can understand that,' says Becky. 'When my Mum started telling me about Dad leaving I wanted to just go away and hide, where I wouldn't have to think about it any more . . . yeah, I can understand

63

that,' she repeats. 'Still, the house is certainly a lot tidier since he left. He lives with Andrea and her family now.'

'Do you see much of him?'

'No,' says Becky flatly. Then she goes on. 'I was supposed to be seeing him this weekend. Then last night he was on the phone, all embarrassed, saying he couldn't invite me "home" as he calls it, after all.'

'Why not?'

'Well, Andrea's very busy decorating the house and she can't do that and look after me. He didn't put it like that of course but that's the reason. Not that I blame Andrea. She's got two daughters and is not terribly interested in another one. It's my dad I blame. He's just so much under her influence. He lets her call all the shots.'

Cathy nods sympathetically. 'Suddenly, you only come second. I feel that with Mum. She said Giles moving in wouldn't make any difference to us. But it has. What Giles wants comes first. He knows it, too. When will you see your Dad now?'

Becky shrugs her shoulders. 'To be honest, I don't care when I see him. I've got Mark, who's like my guardian angel, and Adam. You know Cathy, everything's going so well with Adam I keep thinking there's got to be a catch somewhere. And there is one. Adam's parents. They don't know anything about me yet. What are they like?'

'They've always been quite friendly to me,' says Cathy. 'I think they're all right.'

Becky nods. 'I'm hoping Adam will tell them soon. I'm sure we can win them round.' Cathy wonders if it will be quite as easy as that. But any further discussion is broken up by the arrival of Jason. He takes off his shades and stares around at the place with such undisguised horror that Cathy bursts out laughing.

'Why the hell did you want to come here?' he exclaims, and pulls his shades back on again.

'Because we like it,' says Cathy, smiling.

'I just hope no one saw me come in here,' he says.

'Otherwise your reputation will be ruined, won't it?' teases Cathy.

Jason orders a coffee and, as soon as it arrives, he pulls out of his pocket a tiny bottle of whisky. Then he pours a generous portion of it into his coffee. This is obviously to impress Becky, Cathy thinks. Jason always acts up when new people are present. He offers the bottle to Cathy.

'No thanks, I bet that tastes awful.'

He takes a sip, then smacks his lips the way bad actors do in adverts.

'You don't know what you're missing, Cathy.'

It's at moments like this, Cathy thinks, Jason is just a big kid. But he is also positively charming to the woman serving them. 'I really admire her,' he says. 'I mean, I couldn't work every day in a dive like this.' He gives her a pound tip, too.

Jason hasn't been able to get through to the local press, so while Becky goes on to college, Cathy stops off at the sports shop. She wants to make sure Jason gets through to the papers this time as it will make such a difference if they turn up tomorrow.

Cathy follows Jason into the manager's office, which now looks more like Jason's office. There, on the desk, is his red sombrero, his copy of *Viz*, a couple of video magazines, even one of his life-savings certificates.

'I'll try Anne again,' he says.

Anne is Jason's contact on the Catford Express. Well, he met her once when she wrote a feature on local sab groups and he reckons he can get her to cover the demo at Radleys tomorrow. He picks up the phone, then leans across for his sombrero and tilts it at an angle on his head with his left hand, while dialling with his right hand. 'This hat always brings me luck,' he says. Then, into the receiver, 'Good afternoon, I'd like to speak to Anne Templeton. It's Jason calling.'

Cathy's mum always comments on Jason's voice, and how husky it is. Her mum's right, even though Jason puts it on a bit – like now.

'Hi, Anne, we met at the sabs . . . that's right,'

he winks at Cathy, chuffed Anne remembers him. 'I'm ringing you now with a really big story.' He starts spieling away, swinging back on his chair now, his sombrero leaning against a huge *NO SMOKING* sign. The shop is full of them. But, of course, it isn't enough for Jason to lean against the sign. Even though he's practically given up smoking and is always saying how unhealthy it is, he has to light one up now.

Just like he'd always very carefully tramp across every centimetre of grass that had, 'DO NOT WALK ON THE GRASS' on a notice over it. 'I don't like being told what to do,' he'd say. And that's part of it. But then Cathy sees him looking across at her, just to check she's noticed what a lad he is. After all this time, he still thinks he's got to perform for her. Doesn't he trust her enough to lose some of his camouflage?

'No one knows me,' Jason said more than once. Yet, she has the feeling that one day he will confide in her. One day he will tell her things he's never told anyone else. While she'll sit there, nodding wisely and swearing never to reveal his secrets.

She looks at him a little impatiently. He's currently blowing a huge smoke ring. Then he says, 'Oh, yeah, loads of good picture opportunities. See you tomorrow then, Anne, about eleven o'clock. And if you need to touch base with me before then, I'll be at Cartford 38210, that's Warners Sports

and Leisure Shop, just ask for the acting manager
I'll see you soon. Bye.' He puts the phone down
and grins triumphantly.

'She's coming, then?'

'Sure, no problem. Told her there'd be at least
two hundred people.'

'I don't know if there will be that many.'

'Well, she's not going to count them, is she?'

Cathy gets up. 'Thanks, Jason, this really will
give us vital publicity. Now I'd better go. Grant
can be really sarky if you're late.'

Jason shakes his head. 'Students,' he says loftily.
Then he seems to hear again what she said. 'Grant,
he the guy Lauren's seeing?'

He asks the question so quickly, he nearly
chokes on it.

Cathy's stunned he knows about Grant. 'Who
told you?'

Jason is still leaning back on his chair but now he
has his eyes half closed in his best Clint Eastwood
impression. 'Cathy, I have spies everywhere, you
know that.' There's a pause, then he asks, 'So is
it true, then?' His voice cracks, just a little.

'Well you know how Lauren always wanted to
go to Lombards. So she let him take her there.
And they've been to the cinema. But I don't think
it's anything serious.'

'I just wondered.'

Oh, don't lie, thinks Cathy – you've thought of

nothing else since you heard. You've been wanting to ask me all lunchtime. Should she push it? But whatever you try and do for Lauren and Jason goes all wrong. There's no time to say anything anyway. Just then the door bursts open and the manager is scowling before them. 'What the hell is going on?'

At first Cathy thinks he means the whisky and the hastily stubbed-out cigarette, but then she realises that he is so angry about something else he hasn't even noticed this sin yet. 'My answer-phone is knee-deep in complaints about you. What are you playing at, Jason?'

Jason rises slowly to his feet, the sombrero still on his head.

'How dare you attack a customer in my shop. I've had his parents on the phone and two customers who happened to be in the shop and are never going to come in again while you are here. Well, come on lad, explain yourself.'

The manager is in his early thirties and has a bank manager's face and an athlete's body. He is friendly but rather sharp. You feel those eyes behind the silver framed glasses don't miss much. Yet his manner is always polite, if sarcastic. It is quite a shock to see him so furious, he can't stand still.

'It was a personal matter,' says Jason, his voice flat and low.

'Personal!' exclaims the manager, and his feet

69

are beating so fast now you wouldn't be surprised
if he started tap-dancing with rage. 'But his parents
say the boy didn't even know your name – he
described you all right though. So do you know
the boy you attacked?'

'No.'

'Well, how can it be personal?'

'He insulted one of my friends.'

The manager coughs, 'You've been smoking in
here.'

Cathy watches him take in the state of the office,
– and her.

'Can I help you, young lady?' he asks Cathy.

She gets up. 'No, it's all right, Jason was just
giving me some advice about sports clothes. Now
I know which ones to get. Thanks, Jason.' She
winces at her unconvincing performance.

Jason gives her a quick, don't worry about me,
smile which, under the circumstances, she thinks
is rather brave of him.

She feels bad leaving him, too, when he most
needs moral support. She's also more than a bit
keen to hear about his fight – and who had been
insulted – was it one of them?

She whispers, 'Good luck,' to Jason and throws
a reproachful glance at his sombrero. As she closes
the door she hears the manager say, 'I want a full
explanation before I . . .'

*

70

'So you don't know what Jason's boss is going to do?' asks Mark. He is sitting in a huddle with Cathy and Becky in Grant's classroom.

'No, I had to leave. I'll give Jason a ring at breaktime.'

'He can't sack Jason, though, can he? I mean, Jason's the best assistant he's had,' declares Mark.

'You don't know anything about this fight Jason got himself into, do you Mark?' asks Cathy.

'I was there, actually,' says Mark, more than a little proudly.

'And was it about one of us?' asks Cathy.

'Well, Jason asked me not to tell anyone. So this is in confidence,' whispers Mark.

'Yes, yes,' cry Becky and Cathy together.

'Jason got into a fight with Clive Sturgess.'

'Clive!' exclaims Becky.

'Keep your voice down,' says Mark. 'He's only sitting over there. Anyway, it was Jason who did all the fighting. It was the most amazing thing you ever saw. Clive says something snidey about Lauren and then, wow, kaput . . .'

'What's this gossip?' asks Lauren, suddenly standing over them.

Fortunately, before they answer, Grant appears.

As they go back to their desks, Becky whispers, 'Mark, what are you doing tonight?'

'Don't know yet.'

'Well, why don't you come out with Adam and me tonight, you'll never guess where we're going.'

'Ladies and gentlemen, when you're ready,' says Grant. Then he picks up their essays and lets them fall on to his desk. He doesn't say anything else, just stands staring at their essays, shaking his head. Everyone in the class shifts uneasily. Finally, a voice calls out, 'That bad, are they?'

Grant looks around, his face as solemn as a vicar offering last prayers at a graveside, before hissing, 'Your essays, ladies and gentlemen, had an oddly familiar ring. I felt as if I had read them before and, of course, I had. They were all copies, weren't they? And yet, I asked for your view of *Hard Times*. YOURS. It's all right not to like a classic, you know.' He sighs. The class is hushed, completely still. 'Only two people's essays had a glimmer of originality about them.' he declares. 'One was Clive Sturgess. Your observation about the role of Stephen Blackpool made me think again about my own reading of the book. Well done, Clive.'

Clive takes his essay, his face one big gloat. There are whispers of 'What did you get?' and he mouths 'B+.' Mark notices that Becky deliberately looks away from Sturgess, though.

'I don't often give A- to first years,' continues Grant. 'In fact, I don't often give A- to second years. Yet this essay offered such a stimulating analysis of Louisa Gradgrind, that I had no choice. Well done – LAUREN.'

Lauren jumps forward. She worked hard on that essay but even so she hadn't expected an A-. Especially as her last mark had been B-. Grant is saying something else about her essay but it's hard to hear because there's an outbreak of coughing, or rather a collective throat-clearing. Sharp, nasty, cruel sounds. Little volleys of gunfire aimed straight at her.

Grant puts her essay down on her desk to the accompaniment of a new sound. Lauren turns round. A girl is making another kissing noise on to her hand. The girl she thought she had seen at Lombards.

Lauren feels herself flinch. Grant must have seen the girl too. She wonders if he's going to say something. She hopes not, because, well, what can he say? She tries to look up at him but she can't. She looks down at her essay instead and feels the pulse of her neck beating faster and faster.

Grant walks to the front of his class and starts giving out the rest of the essays, his voice strangely parched now.

'You all right?' asks Cathy.

Lauren nods. Then suddenly she snatches up her essay furiously, as if she's snatching it away from them. She stuffs the essay into her bag, then glares round defiantly at the class. Why should she hang her head in shame because a lecturer enjoys her company. It's not her fault she's sophisticated. But that had nothing to do with her getting an A-. She's good at English, she got an A in English Language and a B in English Literature at GCSE. Anyway, Grant wouldn't mark her up because he's going out with her, would he?

Jez watches Stephen cleaning the side of his till with a cloth. Then he shakes his head gravely. 'He's putting everything he's got into cleaning that till, isn't he?' says Jez.

Cathy's watching him in some amazement too. 'I know, and that's one job I really hate.' For it's down the side of the till where all the food is. Most of the regular staff have gone, leaving what Jez terms, 'the proles' to tidy up the store for tomorrow's visit. Cathy's been cleaning out all the cabinets and Jez is supposed to be sweeping up.

'This fight Jason had,' asks Jez, suddenly. 'You don't know what it was about?'

'Yes, someone slagged off Lauren in the shop,' says Cathy, quickly. Ever since the truth game she's felt distinctly embarrassed even mentioning Lauren to Jez. She shouldn't have just rushed off that night. It must have looked so peculiar.

The first time she saw Jez after the truth game was at Radleys. At first he didn't say anything at all. Then she said something very everyday and he

74

looked so relieved. He said, 'I didn't think you were going to talk to me at first.' Then added, 'I'm really, really sorry if I upset you.' And she said, 'No, you didn't. Don't worry.'

And it wasn't really Jez's fault. It's just he'd disappointed her. She'd known he fancied Lauren – everyone did – and that he had a little crush on her. But never had she guessed he was so obsessed with her. Somehow, she'd imagined him being above that sort of passion. She'd been bowled over by this horrible feeling of being totally out of it and of being unsexy and unfanciable. That's why she decided to buy some new clothes. Yet even while she tried on the blue dress Cathy was annoyed with herself wasting time on such trivia. She'd got so much to do, so many important things. It's just, sometimes she feels totally unimportant. She envies Becky, in a way, having Adam needing her so much. And yet, Cathy doesn't want to be one of those girls who just tag after their boyfriend all the time.

'Still, at least Jason can keep his job,' continues Jez.

'Yeah, but when I rang him he sounded so down – for Jason.' Then she thinks of something else. 'Jez, do you suppose Jason will be able to get away tomorrow to help me?'

'Yeah, of course he will,' says Jez.

'He's my number 2,' says Cathy.

'No, he'll be there all right,' says Jez. 'But even if he isn't, the demo's all planned. Everyone knows to meet outside Radleys at eleven o'clock with their *Meat is Murder* banners, don't they?'

'Yes, that's true.'

'And if there's anything extra you want doing, just ask me.'

Cathy tries to look comforted by this offer. They talk on about tomorrow, Jez being cheerful about it all as only Jez can. Then suddenly Mr Lurie is drooping beside them. Cathy looks up. She's got a certain sympathy for him and normally when he sees her his eyes twinkle just a little. But they're not twinkling now and his voice is grave. 'Mr Fanshaw wants to see you immediately.'

It's then Cathy notices that Stephen isn't cleaning his till anymore. In fact, Stephen seems to have disappeared. But she doesn't have time to think any more about this as she's already being ushered upstairs.

Adam gently ties his scarf round Becky's face.

'There really is no need for this, you know,' he says.

'Oh, yes there is,' she replies. 'For, if anyone gets cross that you brought me here – at least you can say, 'Ah, but she doesn't know the combination of the lock.'

'No one's going to get cross,' says Adam. As he

turns the magic numbers 777 he tuts with annoyance.

'What's wrong?' asks Becky.

'There's a bit of graffiti on our door. I'll have to wash that off.'

Then he leads her into the shed and removes the scarf from her face.

'It probably doesn't look much to you now,' says Adam. 'Really you've got to try and imagine it as it was. Over there, for example, right in the corner was our lino – I bought it, actually – and that's where we'd all crash out. There were a few cushions too and there'd always be a mad rush for those. I had an old cassette player which I left there and Jez kept most of his tapes here, while those walls were full of pictures, you can still see a few of them.' Elderly, curled pictures of Charlie Sheen and Tom Cruise still cling uncertainly to the walls. They look, Becky thinks, like shrivelled-up leaves just waiting to fall. 'Lauren bought most of the pictures. Sometimes we also had a bit of a bar, you can guess who was in charge of that.'

'Yes, I can see Jez mixing up the drinks.'

'Some nights,' recalls Adam, 'we'd have to carry him out of here. He would be out of his skull. We'd take him round Mark's and just fill him with black coffee.'

Becky stares around. 'I suppose you also had torches.'

'Yeah, and one giant flashlight, that was Mark's, I think. But actually we liked it dark. Cathy used to say the dark in here was quite different to the dark in her bedroom.'

'And no one ever spotted you here?'

'Never, not once. After a while we stopped worrying about being discovered. Here, at least, we were shut in safely against the world.'

'And to think all I ever did was go up a friend's treehouse a couple of times.' She then reads aloud. 'This is private property and belongs to Jez, Lauren, Adam, Mark, Cathy and Jason, Blaze.' She repeats 'Blaze' questioningly.

'Jason had two names.'

She smiles. 'A real little gang, weren't you?'

We *were* on the run,' says Adam. 'And if they'd got us . . .'

'They did get Mark didn't they?'

'Mark tell you about that, did he?'

'Yes, poor Mark.'

'He's supposed to be meeting us here tonight,' Adam says, 'but when I rang him, he said he had too much work to do and I didn't like push it.' Ever since Adam started going with Becky, Mark's been elusive. He still chats with Adam but they hardly ever meet up now. He's always busy, or that's his excuse.

'Did you tell your mum you were out with Mark this evening?' asks Becky.

'Yeah, usual excuse.'

'Adam, it's my mum's book-signing next week. Poor Mum, she's terrified no one's going to be there. Anyway, I'd love it if you were able to come to that.' She rushes on, 'And I think it would be a really good time for me to introduce you.' She sees by Adam's face he doesn't agree.

'I'd like to be there,' says Adam slowly. 'It's just my mum will be there too.'

'I know, but I thought if your mum met my mum and realised what a good literary background I came from, that might impress her. Then I could smile sweetly at her and say, 'Hi, how's the coke habit?' She flashes him one of her sudden, dazzling smiles. 'What do you think?'

Adam can't refuse her anything when she looks at him like that. 'Yeah, I'll be there and I'll speak to my mum about us.'

Her face is all lit up now and suddenly Adam feels that anything is possible.


Cathy stumbles back downstairs. How long had she been in Baked Bean's office? It felt like several days and nights.

When she went in he was flicking the switches on his very own starship, Radleys. No one was safe from his gaze. Wherever you were you could suddenly explode into view on one of his screens. He couldn't hear you though, could he? Yet Cathy quickly discovered he didn't need to. He had his own portable ears.

And this spy had told him everything he needed to know about Cathy's demonstration. And even as he roared away at her he kept looking down and flicking switches. Was he showing off? Or did he need these quick fixes of spying, just to prove to himself how powerful he was.

Cathy felt as if she'd been sent to the head-master. At first she could feel herself wilting. She always did when confronted by authority. There was a part of her that wanted to be a good little girl and have all these nice boss-men (and occasionally boss-women) pat her on the head, so when he said that what she planned for tomorrow was in breach of her contract there was a little part of her that wanted to say, 'Oh dear, sorry about that. Yes, I'll cancel everything,' and scurry away, full of apologies that she'd dared disturb the peace of the great god, Fanshaw.

She remembered when she'd been caught smoking her one and only cigarette at school, which she'd hated anyway, and had been sent to the head-master. He obviously thought she was a hardened chain smoker and bellowed away at her while she sat blubbering in the corner, never even trying to explain.

Today, though, she did speak up for herself, declaring that what she did in her own free time was up to her. And tomorrow's demonstration was a mark of personal conscience.

Then he suddenly switched into a much oilier tone, declaring what a very promising assistant she was and how she mustn't throw it all away now. She nearly laughed out loud when he said that. She was just till fodder, they all were. He must be very scared to be trying this routine out on her.

This thought cheered her up so much she stopped arguing with him. Let him think he'd got to her. But as she went back downstairs it hit her again. Fanshaw knows. Her trump card tomorrow had been surprise. Now he was ready. And all because someone of her own age from her old school had run bleating to him with tales.

The informant is cleaning his till again, whistling under his breath as he does so. Upstairs Cathy had felt nothing but hatred for him. Now there's a kind of wonderment too. Why did he do that? She remembered her dad saying that in business you always had to watch your back as there was always someone ready to put the knife in. But that was middle-aged men, jostling for positions of power – not sixteen-year-olds in a grubby old supermarket.

'I hope you feel proud of yourself,' she calls.

He doesn't even look up, just continues whistling. But Jez steams over.

'What's happened?'

81

'Fanshaw knows about the demo because some-one grassed us up. Guess who?'

She calls out again. 'I hope you feel proud of yourself, Stephen.'

'Yes, thank you,' he replies without looking up but in such a bright, I'm so pleased with myself, voice, Cathy is shocked. He might at least sound ashamed of what he's done.

'Want to be promoted, do you?' cries Jez. 'Even if it means grassing people up.'

'No, not at all,' says Stephen.

'So why did you grass Cathy up then?'

Never has a till been scrubbed so vigorously as Stephen is scrubbing it now.

'Because what you're doing is wrong – just because you don't like eating meat.'

'Actually, Stephen,' said Cathy, 'what I was saying to Jez was confidential and none of your business.'

'I think it was my business,' says Stephen. 'What you were planning would have humiliated our shop in front of the chairman. And that might not have mattered to you as you just see this job as a joke but to some of us it's our career.'

Even if she'd seen this job as a career Cathy would have gone ahead with the demo, wouldn't she. It might have been harder, though. She concedes that.

'You wanted to get in with the boss and now you have,' says Jez, 'that's why you did it.'

'And you don't care about all the animals whose lives might have been saved?' says Cathy.

'Chickens,' says Stephen contemptuously. 'Nobody really cares about chickens.'

'I do,' cries Cathy, 'Chickens have the same right to life as any of us.'

'You just want to get your picture in the paper,' mutters Stephen.

Cathy gapes at him in horror. He can't really think that.

'I'll sort him out, three-faced git,' murmurs Jez, ambling right up to Stephen now.

Cathy watches him in some alarm. Surely Jez isn't going to fight Stephen. Baked Bean will see the fight on one of his screens and sack Jez. Also, even against Stephen, she's not sure Jez would win.

'Jez leave it,' she cries.

But Jez doesn't appear to hear. He goes right up to Stephen and growls, 'Stand up.' Cathy's never heard Jez sound so rough. Stephen obeys him, slowly getting up. He's slightly taller than Jez but he's quivering, too.

'Don't you touch me,' he cries.

Jez stares at him for a long moment. Then he raises his right hand into a fist which he waves into Stephen's face before muttering, 'It's lucky for you

I'm mild-mannered or I'd have punched your head off.'

# 4 Serious Obstruction at Radleys

The policeman looks at Cathy, then glares at Jez. 'What are you doing here?' he asks.

'We are protesting peacefully about the sale of meat in Radleys supermarket,' replies Cathy in the bright, reassuring tone she usually reserves for nervous dogs.

The policeman turns to the policewoman standing beside him and murmurs something while keeping his eyes firmly fixed on Jez.

'And what are you intending to do?' asks the policeman in such a flat tone Cathy is sure he's asked this question hundreds of times before.

'We want to blow the whole place up and you with it,' mutters Jez.

Cathy immediately shakes her head at him. She says, 'All we want to do is hand in our petition, which has over one thousand names on it, to the

Chairman at Radleys,' she peers at her watch, 'in twenty minutes' time.'

'I am afraid we have received a complaint that you're causing a serious obstruction to customers,' says the policeman.

A serious obstruction! Cathy has to laugh now. But it's a very dark laugh. For the awful truth is that at twenty-nine minutes to eleven there are exactly five people obstructing. There's three very reliable girls from the animal rights group standing by the trolleys handing out leaflets and there's Jez and herself hovering by the entrance. AND THAT'S ALL.

Yet last night everyone she'd phoned ('Just a little reminder,' she said as she didn't want to sound too pushy) had promised her faithfully they'd really try and come.

But this morning at college when she was rounding people up, all she got were feeble excuses and bad acting: 'Oh, no, is it this Friday? I thought it was next Friday.' One girl even said, 'But it's too cold to do anything today.' Cathy just had to walk away from her, fast.

Lots of other people were hiding from her. Oh, yes, she knew all about that. She was very tempted, in fact, to storm into the girls' loo just to show them that she knew. And then, would you believe, two girls whom she had managed to drag out of college disappeared on the way to Radleys. To make matters worse Cathy suspected they'd slipped into Benny's Beefburgers.

Jez is still convinced more people will turn up. 'You can rely on your friends for a start,' he says. 'And then there are loads of people who feel as strongly as you. No, you wait and see there'll be a big rush just before eleven o'clock. So don't panic, everything's still at the embryo stage.'

Jez loves that phrase, he was always telling teachers his homework 'was still at the embryo stage.' And right now Cathy's clinging on grimly to that phrase. They won't let her down and far more importantly they won't let all those animals down. Will they?

'Right now I want all you people to move across the road,' says the policeman pointing to the block of offices opposite Radleys. A real I'm-in-charge note has entered his voice.

'But no one will see us there,' cries Cathy.

'Exactly,' says Jez. 'That's exactly what you want. Or what your bosses want. And you have to do what the money men tell you, don't you. I bet you've even got a key in your back, all ready for them to wind you up . . .'

'No, Jez,' interrupts Cathy. He's quite enjoying arguing with that policeman. Just like at school when he could argue with teachers for hours about something really petty like wearing trainers. But it isn't helping. She turns to the policewoman, 'I do

87

think it's very biased of you to order us across the road, especially as we're a peaceful demonstration.'

'And no servant of big business is making me move,' announces Jez. 'No way.' And he proceeds to slide down on to the ground in front of the entrance, narrowly missing a collision with an elderly lady carrying a huge basket.

The elderly lady edges nervously round him, only to be leapt on by Cathy, 'Will you take one of these?' she asks, handing her a leaflet.

'Certainly, dear,' she says, folding the leaflet up carefully, then dropping it into her basket.

'Do read it,' Cathy calls after he.

'Now, look,' says the policewoman speaking for the first time. 'We're not unsympathetic to your cause. I'm a vegetarian,' she adds unexpectedly. Cathy looks at her with a new respect and realises with a shock that this policewoman is probably only about three or four years older than her. 'But we can't have you blocking the entrance, which you are doing at the moment, or causing a congestion by the trolleys. She points to the three girls by the trolleys who have copied Jez and are sitting with arms crossed right in front of the trolleys.

'All right, we'll move back a bit,' concedes Cathy.

'Right back,' booms the policeman. Cathy ignores him and gives a faint smile to the police- woman. 'How long have you been a vegetarian?' she asks.

88

'Since I was fifteen,' she says. 'I wouldn't eat meat now if you paid me.'

The policeman says, 'Any trouble and we shall have to ask you to move right away.'

'There won't be any trouble,' says Cathy. She nearly adds there are only five of us, for goodness sake, but doesn't. She just wants the police to go.

'We're only exercising our democratic right to protest peacefully, brother,' Jez calls after the police. Neither of them reply but they don't go far either, just across the road, in fact.

Cathy and the other girls spring into action again, rushing around with leaflets, while Jez searches frantically for a sweet in his jacket. There's always a sweet in one of his pockets. And finally he retrieves a manky old cough sweet which looks as if its got mildew growing on it. Still, Jez is starving.

He sucks it contemplatively and watches Cathy flinging herself about. No one actually refuses to take a leaflet from her. Perhaps because she looks so sincere, with those wonderful melting eyes of hers. But Jez can't help wondering how many will even look at the leaflet, let alone read it.

He's just wondering whether he could dive into Radleys for a bar of chocolate when he sees Stephen peering out of the window at them. For a second he and Jez stare at each other. And Stephen is smiling at them, an I'm-a-nice-guy-really smile.

Is Stephen feeling sorry now? Or does he just want to be in with everyone?

It doesn't matter. Jez remains stony-faced. Yesterday that grinning hyena grassed them up and anyone who does that is strictly a waste of time person. If you haven't got loyalty from someone then you haven't got anything.

'You're not waving your poster in the air.' Cathy is standing over him.

'Correct.'

'Any reason why not, young man?'

'Saving myself for the big moment, Miss.'

'Oh, come on Jez, you picked one of these posters out, which one was it? Yes, here we are, you said this one was excellent.' She holds up a poster which features a huge plate with various animals on it and underneath in black letters urges KEEP DEATH OFF THE PLATE.

'Stop bossing me, Cathy,' he says, but he lets Cathy place the poster in his hand all the same. 'Now shake it about a bit.'

'I beg your pardon.' Then he says, 'Be patient with me. I've just had a shock. Stephen smiled at me.'

'Nice for you. It's going to be fun facing them all tomorrow afternoon.'

'I've got to face them tomorrow morning.'

'Jez, I'm too scared to look. What's the time?'

'Just gone ten to eleven.'

She shakes her head. 'Oh, no, how could they – we're not still in the embryo stage, are we?'

'Oh, yes we are. Don't panic yet. The main thing is have you worked out what you're going to say to his holiness when you give him the petition?'

'Yes, I was rehearsing it at one o'clock this morning.'

'I didn't think you'd had much sleep.'

'Why, do I look awful?'

'No, just a bit pale.'

'The wind kept waking me up. I swear it was sighing right in my ear.'

'What you've got to do now,' says Jez, 'is save your energy. So come on, relax, tell yourself some jokes. Or even better I'll tell you a joke. Oh, here's a good one.' He starts laughing. 'You'll love this. What's pink and hard – '

'Oh, Jez, right now . . .'

'No, come on.'

'All right. I don't know what's pink and hard.'

'A pig with a flick knife.'

Then he laughs so hard that Cathy starts laughing too. 'That's not funny,' she says.

'So why are you laughing, then?'

'I'm laughing at you. You laugh like a seal. Hur, Hur, Hur.'

'I don't,' says Jez, and then he says, 'There you are, two more,' pointing at Becky and Adam walking towards them.

Cathy notices that Becky is wearing Adam's scarf. Was that a present? Or has he just lent her his scarf because it's cold? Boyfriends certainly do have their uses. Trouble is, none of the boys she ever went out with would have done that. In fact, they'd have probably expected Cathy to give them her scarf. Cathy's pleased to see them and yet she feels defensive, too. She knows what they must be thinking.

'Welcome to a most exclusive demo,' she says. 'You haven't seen a spare hundred people anywhere, have you?' Everyone smiles in embarrassment.

'I do like your posters,' says Becky.

'Yeah, most impressive,' says Adam.

'Where's Mark?' asks Cathy, suddenly.

'Oh he had to stop off at the sports shop to see Jason about something,' says Adam.

'There's nothing wrong, is there?' cries Cathy.

'No,' replies Adam. 'I mean, I don't know why he has to see Jason but I'm sure everything's okay.'

Cathy isn't reassured. 'I was relying on Jason being here . . . oh, everything's just getting worse and worse.'

'Look, stop flapping,' interrupts Jez, 'and go and hand out a few more leaflets.'

'Can I help?' asks Becky.

'Oh, that would be great,' says Cathy. She hands her a pile of leaflets. 'Don't feel you have to give all those out. It's just I thought we'd have more helpers.'

'No sign of Lauren?' asks Becky.

'No, this is not really her thing but she said she would turn up,' says Cathy.

Five minutes later Lauren appears. She's wearing a padded denim jacket, new jeans (but then Jez is convinced she only wears her jeans once) and light brown kickers. And she isn't smiling.

'It's bloody freezing,' she announces grumpily to Jez and Adam.

'Yeah, this wind is Radleys' Siberian special, one day only,' says Jez.

'And where the hell is everyone else,' she demands. 'Thought the place would be swarming with people.'

'So did Cathy,' says Adam.

And right then Cathy turns round from her leafleting to call out, 'Hi, Lauren, great you could come.'

Lauren nods, then murmurs, 'She looks awful.'

'Don't say anything to her,' says Jez.

'No, of course I won't,' says Lauren. 'But she's just worked herself into the ground for this. Her eyes are flashing angrily. 'I didn't think any of our English group would turn up – too immature – but what about all the others?'

'Somehow,' Jez says, 'people always bring you down.' Then he suddenly straightens up, 'Hello, there's movement over in the car park.' He hands his poster to Adam. 'I think this could be it, folks. I'll just go and check.' Jez even half-runs. Adam has to smile at this unfamiliar sight, then he asks Lauren, 'Do you want to hold a poster or something?'

'Adam, I can't hold anything until my fingers have thawed out.'

He gazes down at her thick leather gloves but says nothing. Then Jez comes wheezing back.

'Is it him?' asks Adam.

Jez nods, 'In the fastest car you've ever seen.' He rushes over to Cathy who is talking to a tall horsey-looking woman in a heavy black coat. 'Jez,' says Cathy, 'may I introduce Angela Bailey who runs the animal rights group in . . .'

'No time,' interrupts Jez, 'He's arrived.'

Cathy gasps.

'But stay calm,' he adds.

'But Jez, there's no one here,' cries Cathy.

'Oh, I've done very successful demos with only three people including myself,' says Angela briskly. 'No, it's not the size that's important.'

'That's what I'm always saying,' quips Jez. 'Look, Cathy, the most important person is here and that's you.' He gives her hand a quick squeeze, 'So go on, Cathy, this is it. Your moment.'

She gazes round at the demonstration. It doesn't take long. They're not coming, are they? But they

PROMISED. That's the really callous thing. Well, afterwards she'll see them. She'll tell them what she thinks of them. NO, she won't. She'll machine-gun down the lot of them. For someone who's never considered herself the least bit violent she finds this fantasy oddly soothing. She imagines all their bodies heaped on top of each other in a garage, while above them in their blood she's scrawled NO ONE LETS ME DOWN.

'You all right?' asks Jez. He's standing one side of her. Adam's on the other. And there's Lauren right behind her while Becky's still handing out leaflets. 'I'm fine.'

'Do some deep breathing,' says Jez.

'No, I'm fine,' she said, looking straight ahead at the three figures striding towards her. Baked Bean Man is one side, Mr Lurie the other, and in the middle, a large, bulky man sporting an expensive, loose-fitting suit and the most impressive suntan Cathy's ever seen. Either he's just returned from a month in the sun or he spends every night on a sunbed. His skin gleams with such good health that even Baked Bean seems positively anaemic by comparison. He doesn't appear to be the least bit surprised by the demonstration. Instead, he beams round a smile wide enough to swallow Cathy up in one mouthful.

'So what have we here?' he asks. His eyes alight on Jez. Funny how everyone notices Jez first, 'What are you, the new hippies? Some of us can remember the old hippies.' Tense, forced laughter erupts from Baked Bean Man, Mr Lurie and the Chairman's back. It's only then Cathy notices a meek little man carrying a briefcase standing behind the Chairman.

'So what are you?' he asks again.

Jez nudges her and Adam is giving her a you-can-do-it smile. This is it. Don't hesitate now. Hesitate and you've lost. Where had she heard that phrase? Oh, yes, it was from the woman in the self-defence class. Cathy kept hesitating. No wonder, she only attended one class.

'I'd like to present you with our petition.' The words are out before she realises it. But how small and anxious she sounds. More volume. 'This petition contains over a thousand names protesting about the sale of meat in Radleys.' Angela claps this.

'Thank you, my dear,' he says, taking the petition from her. Up close he looks almost shockingly young, certainly younger than Baked Bean Man. Then he turns to face the small crowd that has gathered around. 'Radleys is the family store and we welcome comments from you, our family. If I may call you that.' Jez starts making throwing-up noises. But the Chairman sweeps on, 'Radleys is your store with a wider variety of food than you will find in any other supermarket. And, yes, we will try and stock some food for our vegetarian friends but . . .' he lets off a slow, fat smile, 'many of our customers enjoy eating meat, they need to eat meat and at Radleys . . .'

Cathy can hear this commercial no longer. 'Need,' she echoes. 'No one needs to eat meat.' But he's still smirking at her. So prove it, she tells herself. Show you know what you're talking about. 'What do you get from meat?' she asks, 'Protein, calcium, and iron. Well, we can get all three of these elsewhere from much healthier foods.' She edges nearer him, then turns around to the crowd. 'Did you know that when you die you'll still have on average seven pounds of undigested meat in your system?'

'That's telling him,' whispers Jez who has edged forward too.

'Got to let people have choice,' he says. 'Choice.' He leans on the word, 'Freedom of choice, my dear, that's what's important.'

'Oh, so if I chose to murder you now you'd say that was all right, that was my choice.' That gets a few laughs in the audience but the police are suddenly right behind her. What do they think she's going to do, assassinate him? She looks across at Baked Bean, snorting at her like an angry bull. But the Chairman is still smiling, still patronising her. 'You can't compare the life of a pig to the life of a man, can you?'

'Why, why can't I?' cries Cathy. 'Don't pigs feel pain like us? And who are we to judge a pig's quality of life? I'll tell you something else,' she yells, her heart thumping excitedly. 'I think people who eat meat should at least care about how the animal is killed, and so should the people who sell it.' All her supporters clap this and there's ragged applause from the rest of the crowd too. Then Cathy thrusts a leaflet in front of him which he immediately swats away.

Clearly he feels he's bestowed enough time on the loonies for he declares, 'Thank you very much for your interest in Radleys. As you can see Radleys is interested in all views, however eccentric.' Then in a low hiss he adds, 'I believe you work for us, my dear.' And he stares at her, his eyes on stalks. But then he's back to being a cuddly pantomine character again as he waves at the audience. 'Goodbye, everyone,' he cries, and even shakes a couple of hands. Cathy glares at them. How could those people want to shake his hand. And now there are more of them smiling respectfully up at him. Didn't they hear what she said? 'Good to meet you, good to meet you,' he murmurs over and over.

He's beaming all over his face as he turns to go. 'You were brilliant,' whispers Adam. But Cathy doesn't think she was. Nothing's changed. How she'd like to wipe that suntan off his face. She'd need a pickaxe.

'Goodbye, everyone,' he calls again, and is just moving away when a voice calls over to then. 'Don't move. Don't move anyone.' A voice Cathy instantly recognises. Everyone whirls round. 'I want just one minute of your time.'

And there is Jason at one end of a large cardboard picture with Mark at the other. Jason is wearing one of his favourite T-shirts. It features a fox putting two fingers up. A number of people are following behind them, curiously, while there's a definite ripple of interest from the crowd. As they get nearer, Cathy can see the cardboard picture is of a pig, while behind the picture are what looks like wires. What are they up to? And then she thinks she knows.

They stop and even though he can be heard perfectly clearly without it Jason is talking through his megaphone again, 'Ladies and gentlemen, this is a picture of a pig before the humans get him.' It's a beautifully drawn picture, must have taken hours. And it looks so real, Cathy thinks. It seems to jump off the cardboard at you.

'And this,' called Jason, through his megaphone, 'is the same pig after the humans have got him.' He nods at Mark who moves some wires round the back of the poster. At first it seems like nothing is going to happen but then suddenly blood or what looks eerily like blood comes trickling out of the holes. And then Cathy notices there are little holes right across the pig's neck and blood is coursing out of every one of them. It is like a huge gash and it just looks so obscene, so ugly. And the ugliness goes on spreading, until it wipes out the pig and all that's left is blood. A little boy starts to cry and his mother carries him away yelling, 'It shouldn't be allowed.' But more and more people are clustering round and staring.

Then Mark picks up the wreath which has been hanging over the side of the picture and stands in front of the crowd, his head bowed. Next Jason steps forward and stares at the crowd, his eyes full of contempt. Out of his pocket he pulls a small packet of coins, then throws the coins on the ground. Everyone of the coins is smeared with blood. Jason and Mark stare at the coins, then look up and point accusingly at the crowd.

And everyone is so hushed, that the sound of someone pushing a trolley is positively deafening. The next sound is applause, thunderous applause which just goes on and on.

It's then Cathy sweeps round to see the Chairman's reaction. Let him smirk his way out of this. But he's gone. Just when did he slip away? Not that it matters. She never thought she'd convert him. She just hoped he'd see how people reacted when they were faced with what really went on. Then she spotted Becky and Angela furiously handing out leaflets. And Cathy is picking her

100

leaflets up when Jez whispers, 'Jason wants you.' Jason is beckoning to her, and standing beside Jason is a guy with a camera round his neck and a girl who is probably the reporter. The reporter is looking really animated. And people are just lapping round that poster now.

It's all due to Jason, of course. She doubts if anyone will remember her carefully rehearsed speeches. But still, what does that matter. Today isn't an ego trip for her. Now Jason is shaking her by the hand and so solemnly she wants to laugh. He's such a showman. And then Mark shakes her hand, his face an exact copy of Jason's. 'Both of you were brilliant,' she enthuses. They try and look modest.

Then Jason introduces her to the reporter as 'the mastermind behind today', and she is posing for pictures with Jason and Mark. She beckons to Jez and Adam and Angela to join her but they all just smile and shake their heads, Jez mouthing, 'No way.' And there, right in the back of the crowd, she sees her mum. Her mum raises her thumb smiling shyly. She and her mum haven't been getting on so well lately. It's Giles' fault, of course. And even when he's not physically there he's still polluting the air. She drinks in the sight of her mum, on her own, without him and then Lauren is saying, 'Well done, Cathy. I was really proud of you,' but her eyes are on Jason. She so wants to

101

get Jason's attention too. So she says loudly, 'And the poster was brilliantly effective.' He turns round and bows slightly. 'Thank you,' he says. And Lauren wants to say something else, something to bring him closer to her because she feels hundreds of miles away from him.

Not like the last time he was being congratulated. It was when he won that country swimming trophy and there were even more people round him then, patting him on the back. But all the time his eyes were scanning the crowd for her. And she remembered pushing her way through that crowd and him helping her up on stage where she stood right beside him, where she belonged – and where she belongs now. But then she sees another girl weave her way over to Jason, an attractive – well, moderately attractive, girl with blonde hair just a tiny bit like Lauren's.

'Who's that?' she asks Cathy.

'Tania, she just started working part-time at the sports shop.'

'Oh, has she?' says Lauren, and then to change the subject Lauren declares, 'I'm going to turn vegetarian.'

'Oh, Lauren, that's great,' cries Cathy.

'Yes, I've decided. I mean I'll still eat fish, of course,' she stops.

Cathy is staring at her, horrified. 'But why? Fish are the most peace-loving animals in the world.

They just swim round, not hurting anyone. And in a way it's worse eating fish than a cow. For you're only eating a part of a cow while you're eating a whole fish, a whole life destroyed just for you.'

'Oh right, I see,' murmurs Lauren, heartily wishing she hadn't said anything. Meanwhile, Becky and Adam are standing with Mark, examining the wires at the back of the poster. 'And then you pulled those wires and the jar tipped forward,' says Becky, 'and what was the blood really?'

'Red dye, my idea,' replies Mark. 'As was the wreath.' He grins at them, positively flushed with success.

'It's all really effective,' cries Becky. 'And this was why I couldn't go out with you last night,' continues Mark. For it all had to be top secret. Sorry I couldn't tell you anything about it, Adam,' he adds. Adam doesn't reply.

He's not sure if Mark is intending to irritate him but he is. Why on earth couldn't he tell Adam, his best mate? They're on the same side, for heaven's sake.

Jason taps Mark on the shoulder. 'Look, I've got to shoot off,' he says. Tania is standing beside him. 'All right if I leave you in charge of this?'

'Certainly,' says Mark. 'Tania reckons we should do this again in the town centre on Saturday.'

Jason frowns, 'No, we've done it now. We'll do something else on Saturday.'

'Oh yeah, that's right,' agrees Mark at once.

Adam shakes his head. Sometimes it's quite pathetic the way Mark's so desperate to play Robin to Jason's Batman.

'Got any spare leaflets?' Jason asks Becky.

'You can take what's left of mine,' she says. Becky is walking with Jason and Tania when Cathy speeds over.

'Jason, I never asked you about your boss,' cries Cathy, 'was he all right about you having an early lunch. You haven't been sacked or anything?'

'*Me* sacked?' cries Jason. 'Impossible.'

'Talk about ego,' says Tania, but she says it in quite an affectionate way, Cathy thinks. And Cathy finds herself wondering if there is something going on between Jason and Tania. Tania's got a definite look of Lauren about her. And then she sees Lauren hovering a little way from them. 'Actually, the boss was really nice to me this morning,' says Jason. 'And I couldn't work out why, because yesterday, well, he wasn't exactly disco-dancing.'

'You can say that again,' murmurs Tania.

'But today he's all matey with me and just as I'm leaving to come here he says, "By the way Jason, I know that fight was over a girl."'

Lauren pricks up her ears at this. What fight? What girl? She edges forward a bit closer.

'So who told him?' asks Cathy.

'I don't know,' says Jason. 'Tania says he was

104

pumping everyone in the shop for info yesterday. But anyway he puts his arm on my shoulder and he says to me, "I still condemn what you did but I applaud your motives." Jason shakes his head. 'Still, as I've already had an hour and a half for lunch I'd better go.' Cathy gives him a quick hug. 'Thanks Jason,' she says. 'I was so worried you wouldn't be able to make it.'

Jason looks shocked. 'But you had my word I'd be here.' Then he nudges Cathy, 'Look at old Jez.' Jez is sitting on the office steps, his sign by his feet, hunched over a cigarette. 'He says he's exhausted,' says Cathy. 'Poor Jez.' She, Jason and Tania walk over to him while Becky goes back towards Adam and Mark.

'Er, Becky,' Lauren calls. Becky stops. Lauren knows she is going to regret asking this but there's something inside her just crying to know. 'That fight Jason was in, was it over her,' she nods to Tania.

'No, it was over you,' says Becky promptly, certain that Lauren must have known already. But just one glance at Lauren's face proves that she hadn't. She just stands gaping at Becky then very quietly asks, 'Please tell me exactly what happened.'

# 5 *Becky Learns the Truth*

Cathy's still breathing in gasps. She's run faster than she has in years. And she's not sure exactly why. Somehow she felt she had to be here. Yet she doesn't know what she's going to say to Jez. What can she say?

She steadies herself by the wall outside his house, then walks quickly up the driveway. Best not to think too much about what she's going to say. She rings the doorbell and almost instantly Jez's mother appears. She's wearing an apron over her skirt and dull green slippers but her blouse has a little red bow on it and her hair is, as always, very 'done'.

'Hi, Mrs Stephens, is Jez in?' Cathy tries to sound light and everyday. Funny how difficult that is now.

Cathy stands inside the hallway. Normally Jez's

mum would sprint off and call up the stairs to Jez. But today she doesn't. Instead she stands over Cathy sending a strange mixture of perfume and disinfectant wafting up her nostrils.

'You know he's been sacked,' Jez's mum says suddenly.

Cathy flushes guiltily. 'Yes, I just heard. I rushed over here as soon as I heard.' She waits for Jez's mother to blame her. If she hadn't made Jez go on that demo with her . . .

But Jez's mum just sighs, 'Wasn't much of a job, I suppose.'

'No' agrees Cathy.

'But still,' she sighs again. 'He's in his room, love, you go on up. I think he's a bit down,' she adds, confidingly. Cathy's positively blazing with guilt now.

Outside Jez's room Cathy can hear music. Is it Pink Floyd? She should recognise their stuff. Jez plays it often enough. She knocks gently on the door. No answer. Then she knocks considerably louder. Still no answer.

She eases open the door. The curtains are drawn and the room is in total darkness except for one candle in a wine bottle. She could be visiting an invalid, if it weren't for the smell of incense and the fact that Jez is lying, fully clothed, save for socks, on top of his huge double bed, which consumes three quarters of the room.

**107**

'Jez.'

He wiggles a toe.

'Are you all right?'

'I'm just mellowing out,' he says, then drops back on to his pillow again. But he waves his left hand at her. 'Come and join me,' he says. Then he looks up and grins, 'Best offer you'll get this week.'

It would seem rather prim, if she didn't, Cathy decides. So she takes her shoes off and then jumps on to the bed beside him.

'That's a lot cosier, isn't it?' he murmurs. She doesn't answer for a moment, just lies staring up at all the photographs on the ceiling. Every inch of that ceiling is crammed with pictures of people Jez admires. So The Damned rub shoulders with Ghandi – and Harry Secombe. Harry Secombe. That must be one of Jez's little jokes.

'Jez, I heard about your job,' she says at last, 'I'm so sorry.'

'And I was only seven minutes late,' says Jez bitterly. 'Earliest I've been since I started. I said, "I'm sorry I'm a bit late but I had a dream about the F.A. cup final and it went to extra time." I thought a little joke might lighten the atmosphere a bit, as everyone was looking at me so oddly, like I had a contagious disease. Anyway, Baked Bean Man was waiting for me in his chamber of horrors. And he was just so gleeful about it all. That's the word – gleeful. The staff weren't, though, they said they'd miss me. I shook hands with a few of them before I was flung out.' A sudden thought hits him. 'But what are you doing here? You should be . . .'

'I resigned.'

'Why?'

'Well, I couldn't go on working there after you'd been sacked.'

'But that's what Baked Bean Man wanted, both of us out, and you've given it to him on a plate.'

'I'll tell you something though, Jez,' says Cathy. 'Before I left I went round stabbing all their frozen chickens with my pen.' Jez starts laughing.

'What are you laughing at?'

'You – you crack me up,' he laughs again. But then he asks, 'So what are you going to do now?'

'Oh, I'll get another job somewhere.'

'Yeah, I can just see ya behind the perfume counter smashing all the bottles that aren't cruelty-free.'

Cathy smiles. 'But it's you Jez, I'm worried about – what are you going to do?'

Jez stretches. 'Actually, Cathy, I'm what you might call semi-retired now.' He stretches again.

Cathy stares at him. 'Semi-retired at seventeen?'

'That's right. Look Cathy, the truth is, I'm not cut out for work. It's like – well, you know some people can't eat sprouts, Cathy. You bung them on their plate and they know they're just teeming with

109

vitamins but they just can't eat them. Other people can't . . .'

'Eat carrots.' prompts Cathy.

'If you like, but everyone's got something they can't do – and mine's work. I mean, I'll do a bit of work here and there for money,' he adds, 'but that's all.'

'But Jez, won't you get bored just sitting about?'

'No, I can sit about for days doing nothing very happily. Anyway, what's so great about working? How many people spend their lives doing the same thing over and over again? And what else is there to do? Be one of those people who spend all their time watching stocks and shares and waving phones around. Or go and join one of those stiffs in parliament who think they're so wonderful. If they knew that millions of people are sitting at home laughing at them – if they haven't switched them off altogether.'

'All right, all right,' interrupts Cathy, knowing Jez can go on like this for hours. 'But come on Jez, there must be one job you'd like.'

Jez pauses, then sits up, 'This is going to sound silly.'

Cathy sits up too. 'No, come on, tell Auntie Cathy.'

'Well, auntie, it's like this. I'd like to own my own sweet shop.'

Cathy is about to laugh until she sees that, for

110

once, Jez isn't smiling. 'It would be a tiny little shop in the country with cobblestones outside and inside as far as you could see there'd be jars and jars of sweets. And when you come in, you'd say, "A pound of pear drops and a pound of jelly beans, please," and I'd say, "Well, I'll just put them on the scales for you, my lovely." ' Jez is speaking with a heavy Devon accent now. 'Then the door would open again and I'd say, "Oh, morning, Milkie, I've put your liquorice by and there's your paper – all the papers in my shop would be a day late, by the way.'

'That figures,' smiles Cathy.

'And then I'd say, would you like a cup of tea, with full Devonshire cream, best in these here parts, they do say. I'd also have a little tea shop, just two or three tables . . .' he pauses, then in his normal voice he says, 'You can laugh, if you like.'

'Oh, Jez I think it's wonderful and frankly I can just picture you weighing up the sweets in your old brown coat. Listen, if I ever come into some money I'll give you some to put down on that shop.'

'Just a tiny one, mind,' says Jez, 'and if possible with an old country pub next door.'

Cathy looks across at him and for a minute she feels like – well, this sounds absurd, but she feels like they're an old married couple. And perhaps he feels that too, for it's then he kisses her very gently on the lips. It's the way Cathy imagines people

kissing in nineteenth-century novels. And it is surprisingly refreshing.

'What was that for?'

'Oh, I just like to keep in practice,' says Jez.
Then there's a rather embarrassed silence broken
by Cathy sniffing.

'What's that smell?'

'Probably the candle, it's scented.'

'No, it's a cheese and onion smell.' She sniffs
again. 'Some people's armpits smell of cheese and
onion but I don't think it's your armpits – it's your
feet.'

'My feet don't smell.'

'Oh, Jez they reek.'

Jez indignantly raises his right foot and then
starts slowly moving it over to Cathy. 'This foot
doesn't smell,' he says.

Cathy screams, 'Oh, yes it does,' Then as the
foot looms nearer she cries, 'Oh, don't Jez,' and a
bright light lands on her, lands on both of them.

Jez's mum stands in the doorway. 'Just thought
I'd see if you wanted any tea,' she says.

'Oh, yes please,' mumbles Cathy.

'Yes, great Mum,' says Jez. As soon as she's
gone Jez breaks into a great roar of laughter.

'Sssh, she'll hear you,' says Cathy, 'and what
must she think of me, only up here two minutes
and . . . what do you think she thought we were

112

doing? Oh, stop laughing Jez. I bet she thought I was a right hussy.'

'Hussy,' echoes Jez. And now Cathy is laughing too. And anyway, she thinks she'd rather be thought a hussy than 'a nice girl'. Surely that's the most damning phrase in the English language: 'a nice girl'.

'I've just had an incredible idea,' says Jez. 'Why don't you go home, wash your feet and then we'll go out and blow my last week's wages on a meal out. I figured you'll be cheap to feed. You'll probably be happy chomping away on a carrot, won't you?' He pauses. 'You look stunned.'

'Yes, I am a bit. You mean, just us two go out for a meal?'

'Yes, unless you think we need a chaperone.'

Cathy's both excited by this offer and alarmed. 'But I can't let you pay for me.'

'All right, you pay for me, then.' Jez is grinning but he's also a little tense. So is Cathy. She feels, as if suddenly, they've reached a turning and they're about to set off up a road they've never been on before. And she hasn't a clue where this road will lead to.

'Well, this hesitation is very flattering,' says Jez.

'No, I'm not hesitating.' It's then Cathy remembers something. 'Only I'm due at an animal rights meeting this evening, to report on the demonstration.'

'A likely tale.'

'No, I am Jez, honestly.' She could skive off the meeting. But no, she can't do that. They're relying on her to be there. It's important. It's just that Jez is looking so hurt. 'Another time though,' she says.

He doesn't reply at first. Then he gets up and says, 'All right, clear off to your meeting then.'

She gives an uneasy laugh. 'Being chucked out, am I?'

'That's right.'

'I really do have to be at this meeting. You can ring up the college and check if you like.' He doesn't answer. She picks up the tray and puts the cups on it. 'I'll take this down to your mum.' She starts to open the door with her left hand, while balancing the tray with her right hand. 'Bye, then,' she says.

'Cathy.'

'Yes.'

Jez sits up. 'Out on that demo yesterday you were pretty good. Just thought you'd like to know.' He flops back down again.

'Thanks, Jez, and you were a great help.' He doesn't reply and his eyes appear to be tightly closed. 'I'll see you soon,' she says.

The DJ's voice crackles over the microphone. 'Ladies and gentlemen, your attention please. Master Michael Winters will now take the floor

114

with his mother.' Then the band starts playing a waltz and to rapturous applause Master and Mrs Winters stumble around the floor together.

Adam watches them with a mixture of amusement and horror. That first dance with your mother in full humiliating view of everyone, how well he remembers that from his *barmitzvah*. And it just goes on and on, or so it seemed then. But at least everyone is watching it in a jovial, indulgent mood, clapping and cheering each faltering step. And now finally the boy's father and sister step on to the floor. Other couples follow. And Michael Winters retires, sweating visibly.

Your *barmitzvah* is a good day, though. And even now Adam feels oddly grateful for it. There's a tap on his shoulder, 'Come and say hello to your Uncle Lew and Aunt Joan.' His father is smiling up at him. Adam's been saying hello to dimly remembered relations and answering the same mind-rotting questions all evening. He wishes he could just hand round tapes.

Uncle Lew and Auntie Joan. He stayed with them once, didn't he? He vaguely remembers a huge garden and planting seeds.

As soon as Uncle Lew sees Adam he steps back in exaggerated amazement. 'This giant can't be Adam,' he exclaims. 'Why, I'm looking up at you, you must be . . .' he pauses questioningly.

'Six foot something,' mumbles Adam. It's both

embarrassing and oddly exhilarating to be suddenly peering down at your relations' bald patches. Still, although he's grown a bit he's certain Uncle Lew's done some serious shrinking too.

'You'll have to watch yourself,' cries Uncle Lew, winking at his dad. Uncle Lew was always winking at people, a dapper little man in a loud check suit.

'But he's a good boy, aren't you,' coos Auntie Joan, stretching up her now puffy face for a kiss. Her breath smells of soggy digestive biscuits. 'You always wanted to help me in the garden, don't expect you remember that,' she says.

'Oh, yes, I do,' says Adam politely, and he does, a little.

'You loved planting seeds – always wanted to plant my seeds for me,' she smiles fondly. She was kind to him when he was younger. They both were. But suddenly seeing them again all these years later it's difficult to know how to react to them. They don't seem quite real any more.

'I just can't believe how much he's grown,' cries Auntie Joan. This is clearly Adam's main achievement and it's difficult to know what he can say about it. But then he's not supposed to say much, he's more of an exhibit, really.

Uncle Lew turns to Adam's dad, 'What have you been feeding him, and got any left for me?' There is hearty laughter all around at this comment and then Uncle Lew grows more serious. 'And are you doing A levels, Adam?' Now there's a question he's only been asked ninety-six times this evening. Adam recites which A levels he's doing.

Uncle Lew smiles approvingly. 'Good boy, you can't have too much education, can you?'

'And you're a birthday boy soon, aren't you?' says Auntie Joan. A birthday boy. Adam shudders inwardly. She used to say that when he was about four and it embarrassed him even then. But he just nods and says, 'That's right.'

'Getting any special presents?' she asks.

Adam looks at his dad, who smiles broadly. 'Well, it's all top secret,' says Adam's dad, 'but he could be getting a motorbike.'

Actually, Adam knows he's getting a motorbike, his brother Reuben told him. His parents even asked Reuben which motorbike would be best for Adam – and Rueben knows absolutely nothing about motorbikes. Luckily Reuben rang Adam to get all the info, then passed this on as his expert opinion. And next month Adam should have a secondhand Kawasaki 125cc.

Adam feels a rush of excitement and impatience just thinking about it. And it's incredibly generous of his parents – even though Adam will be paying off half of it by doing odd jobs. But isn't it just so typical of them to assume Reuben was the oracle on everything, even motorbikes.

Reuben and Mum are coming over now. As

Adam watches Reuben smiling his way through the crowd he can't help wondering exactly why Reuben is here, for Reuben knows Michael Winters even less well than he does. So why come all the way up from Cambridge for his *barmitzvah*. Surely he'd have much rather gone out somewhere with his mates. But from the little Reuben says about Cambridge it would seem he hasn't made many friends yet. And he certainly hasn't got a girlfriend. Adam's well ahead in that area.

Now Reuben is presented to Uncle Lew and Auntie Joan. 'I'd know you right away,' says Auntie. And, actually, Adam doubts if Reuben has changed very much from when they last saw him. The same neat haircut, the same open, almost innocent look. Not even university seems to have changed that. It's part of his charm and yet it's also just a little eerie.

How easily, how smugly, Reuben fits in with everyone. Unlike Adam, who's always felt at a distance from all this. But then, Adam's strictly a background person here.

'Do you recognise this lovely lady?' asks Auntie Joan suddenly.

A girl in a white ballgown is swishing rather self-consciously towards them.

'It's Jill,' says Reuben at once.

'That's right,' says the girl, her eyes firmly fixed on Adam. Now he remembers her. Or rather that

118

sulky mouth. She always had to have her own way. And her parents seemed to spend most of their time humouring her.

He gazes at the white ballgown and then for a moment he sees someone no one else can see. Someone who wore an almost identical ballgown at his *barmitzvah*. Often, in dreams, Lisa'd suddenly appear in that ballgown and he'd say delightedly, 'So you're not dead after all.' And then she'd laugh. Like now. Only that's not her laugh, that's Becky's laugh.

Jill says nervously, 'I only asked if you remembered me?' She thinks he's staring at her. How can he explain that he was, in fact, looking through her, to what exactly? He blurts out, 'I'm sorry, your dress reminded me of someone,' and then he winces. It'll seem as if he's asking for sympathy. The sympathetic murmurs dutifully start up at once, while Jill says, 'But of course,' and turns quickly away from him.

'Will you excuse me?' he says. As he walks away he hears, 'He still hasn't got over her, then. It hits the youngest the hardest.' He's glad he can't hear any more.

He joins a small queue by the bar. He just wants to hide away somewhere. He lowers his head and sees his mother.

'You all right, son?'

'Fine.'

119

'Good.' She seems to sense he doesn't want to talk and just taps his arm, 'Everyone's been telling me what a handsome son I've got.' She taps his arm again. 'I say, one day he'll find another girl, when he's ready.'

She's anxious about him, isn't she? Well, she needn't be. Mum, I've found someone. Just four little words. How easy it would be to say them. He wants to tell her. And much as he hates to admit it, he wants her approval. But then she says, 'Oh, look, there's poor Anna, I must go and talk to her.' And right away the words scramble back into his mouth and Adam knows those four words must not be allowed to escape.

He watches his mum go over to 'poor Anna'. For a long time – and even after the death of her husband – she was just called Anna. Then came the discovery that her son was seeing a non-Jewish girl and had got her pregnant. He remembered creeping downstairs and hearing his parents trying to comfort Anna, while she wept about the shame of it all. Later, her son left home with 'that girl' and 'poor Anna' hasn't spoken to him and 'that girl' since.

Adam's mum has been one of the kindest, one of the most supportive. Yet, somewhere in all this solicitousness, Adam can't help sensing relief, too: thank goodness this is happening to someone else, not me. But it is happening to you, Mum. How

120

will you react when I tell you. You'll be tight-lipped at first and you'll recite hourly, 'This is just a phase.' All the time you'll be watching us together, willing it to end. And then you'll start to get desperate. Will you try and send me off somewhere, like poor Anna did with her son. At one time Anna's son was even going to come away with us to America. Adam's dad even offered to pay his fare. Where will you send me, Mum and Dad? And how many nice Jewish girls will you introduce me to before the last stage; that's when everything will become very nasty.

Not just for him but for Becky. BECKY – What am I doing to you? At the moment you're quite enjoying all this secrecy. You told me that, two nights ago. That was when we sneaked out early one morning to go to the hut.

They're meeting up in the hut again tonight. But Becky still thinks this secrecy is only temporary. Any day now she's expecting an invitation for tea and biscuits with his mum.

And that's one invitation she'll never get. You could say he's deceiving Becky, stringing her along. She deserves better than that. It's time he told her.

It's just after two o'clock in the morning when Adam puts on his tracksuit. Then he decides to jam his bedroom door. He ties a piece of string round his door handle and then ties the other end round the headboard of his bed. Now, in what book did someone do that? When he was younger, he was always reading about kids who, in the dead of night, would climb out of windows and rush off to a deserted cottage where they'd catch a gang of desperate villains, much to the consternation of the local police. ('We'd been after that gang for years.')

'BREAKOUT', that's what one of the stories was called. He suddenly feels as if he's leapt into that story: Adam's Breakout. He's always thought that he could be quite an adventurous person. The trouble is, no one else shared that view. Even to his closest friend, he was just good, old, steady, reliable Adam. But Becky doesn't see him like that. She sees deeper than anyone else. Then, with a speed which surprises even himself, he is out of his bedroom window and climbing on to the porch below. Seconds later he's jumped off the porch and on to the garden. Now comes the tricky part. If he moves just a step or two forward he will set off the security lights. So he sneaks round the edges of the garden and springs over the fence with a burst of agility that would have stunned his P.E. teacher.

Becky is waiting in her porch for him. And just seeing her there makes Adam feel both happy and depressed. It's as if he's looking at a scene that is already in the past. For Adam has decided that he must tell Becky the truth tonight, so this is the last time he'll see her like this.

'Come inside for a second,' she hisses. 'I've got something for you.'

He waits in the hallway until she returns with a blue and yellow shirt.

'I saw it in Maceys and thought, Adam.' She holds it up to him. 'What do you think?'

He's quite stunned by this sudden gift. 'Great. But let me pay you for it.'

'No, no, that's okay, early birthday present if you like. You will wear it?'

'Definitely.'

Her face is one huge smile now. 'Anyway, we'd better go, Mum keeps popping out from the shed for more coffee.'

'Got your key somewhere safe?' he asks.

Last time she thought she'd lost her keys and they'd had several minutes of pure panic.

After she's checked this, they set off. It's freezing cold and their breath hangs in the air like small clouds. But everything seems wonderfully fresh too and Adam enjoys the way the grass crunches under their feet. What he enjoys most though, is the stillness. It's just like when your footprints are the first to cut through a field of snow. For a moment it seems as if the rest of the world is on hold. And everything belongs only to you.

As soon as they reach the hut Becky is exclaiming over all the things he'd brought yesterday: a pillow, a radio, a cassette player, a bottle of wine, a bottle-opener, two mugs, more candles and a packet of chocolate biscuits. He opens the wine while Becky gets warm under the blankets. Then Adam decides he needs to get warm too. And they snuggle down, their bodies pressing tightly together.

'Do you think this is what they mean by a love-nest?' murmurs Becky.

Adam laughs. Never has he felt more safe, more secure.

Finally they get up, each now wearing a blanket. Adam hands Becky a mug of wine.

'Make a toast,' she says.

'All right, a toast to . . .' he's about to say, 'to us' but then decides that sounds corny, so instead, he says, 'To our first house.' He laughs as he says it, and so does Becky, but she repeats the toast. 'Shall we crack open the chocolate biscuits. I'm starving,' says Adam.

'And I'm on a diet – from tomorrow.' Becky grabs two chocolate biscuits.

'How about some music?' he looks at her. 'I've never really asked you what kind of music you like.'

'Oh, most kinds really.'

'You don't like hip-hop, do you?'

'I don't mind it.'

Adam shakes his head. 'It's not music, real

music, and the people who like it have a really bad attitude.' He pauses. 'You don't like Vanilla Ice, do you?'

'Oh, yes. Definitely. Do you?'

'I hate and despise Vanilla Ice. I hate most music in the charts, in fact.'

'So, what sort of music do you like then?'

'Music on independent record labels.'

'Oh, right.' she grins. 'You're a bit of a music snob, aren't you?'

'No.'

'Yes, you are.'

'I like some commercial stuff. Guns'n'Roses, for instance. I've got one of their tapes here.'

'Oh, great, put that on and next time I'll bring my Vanilla Ice tape.'

'I'll be out of that door if you do,' mutters Adam.

Becky smiles to herself. Some people take music far too seriously. Still, she'll enjoy teasing Adam. She had a good mind to go through her tapes and bring round things like Jive Bunny – she's certain he'll hate that.

They sit down again. 'Have a pillow,' says Adam.

'Oh, thanks.'

'So what did you do this evening?' he asks.

'Not a lot. I rang up Mark but he said he was going out for a bachelor night out with Jason and some other guys. What exactly is that?'

'It's basically a group of guys sitting round seeing

125

who can laugh loudest at Jason's jokes.' He stops. That sounds as if he's putting Jason down and he doesn't mean to. He's got a lot of time for him. It's just some people's attitude to Jason that irritates him. Like Mark, his best mate. Lately he really has to keep reminding himself of that fact. Why is that? What exactly is going wrong between them. Well, nothing he can put his finger on. There certainly haven't been any big rows or anything. They still chat about football, music and motorbikes, like they always did. And yet it is different. Something good is quietly leaking away. There's a sense of strain, too. Adam's always just a little on edge with Mark now. Suddenly, talking to his best mate is hard work.

'And then,' continues Becky, 'I rang up Cathy. Only she'd already gone out to a meeting. And then I tried Natalie, a girl I know from keep fit, only she was going out with her boyfriend.'

'Boyfriend.' Adam pounces on the word. Most girls would have gone out with their boyfriends tonight. That's what Becky should have done, not sneaked out in the middle of the night to sit in some freezing old hut. He gazes around. Everything suddenly looks so primitive. 'So what did you do in the end. Just stay in?'

Becky gazes up, startled. His tone is almost rude. 'Yeah, I stayed in and watched a terrible film on television about . . .'

126

He gets up, fists, clenched, fighting back tears of frustration. Here it comes now, the full guilt trip again. Just like he'd had at the *barmitzvah*. He'd planned to tell her about his parents on the way home after enjoying this time together first. But now he realises that was just a cop-out, a way of putting off telling her. And that isn't fair to her. She shouldn't be sitting in on her own on a Saturday night. All he's doing is messing up her life. Why he can't even go to her mother's book-signing next week. He's glaring at her now.

'What's wrong, Adam?' she asks.

'I think we should finish.'

'What?' she gasps.

'Yeah. I think you should go out with someone else, someone who can take you out on Saturdays . . .'

'Adam, I didn't mean . . .'

'No, I want us to finish. That's what I really want.' The words are just ripping out of him now, tearing his insides as they go. And she's looking at him with such bewilderment, such hurt. The pain makes him shout, 'I've been wanting to end this for a while.'

'You have?' Becky can hardly speak. It's as if she's suddenly run out of air. All she can do is gasp, breathlessly. What's happened? What's gone wrong? Adam doesn't want to end it, does he? This isn't the brush-off, is it? But then boys are so cowardly about ending things. And their cowardice makes them cruel. The last boy she'd gone out with just stopped returning her calls. No goodbyes, no thanks for the good times. In the end it was his mum who told her, pity just dripping off her voice. She thought Adam was different from other boys.

He is different.

He stares at her, shaking. There's so much anger inside him he can't control it. For he's lost Becky, hasn't he? Just as surely as if she'd died. She's gone, too. He closes his eyes and holds his head in his hands. Suddenly his body feels heavy as if he were being dragged down, way down, to that living hell in the days and weeks after he lost Lisa. He's going back there again. She's left him, hasn't she?

He feels a touch on his shoulder. Her hand feels very cold. She's freezing isn't she thinks Adam with another surge of guilt. She doesn't say anything but her arm wraps itself around him. Tears start invading his face. He can't stop them. 'I'm sorry,' he mutters brushing them away. 'I'm sorry.' And then he lets himself be guided on to the blankets, Becky's arm still tightly wrapped around him. He sniffs.

'I never cry,' he says.

'So I see,' whispers Becky. And there it is, that understanding in her voice again. He looks up. 'You're pretty special,' he says.

128

'I know.'

'But there's something I've got to explain to you about my parents.'

'What's that?'

'My mum is never going to agree to you and me going out together because you're not Jewish. You see, the Jewish line is maternal. So if a man marries a non-Jewish girl the line is lost forever,' his voice is remarkably calm but his heart is racing. 'Do you follow that?'

'I think so.'

'So if my parents knew about us they'd do everything they could to break us up. They'd see it as their duty.'

'Even if they liked me?'

'It wouldn't matter. There's nothing you could do, absolutely nothing. They'd see you as their enemy.'

There's a long moment of silence, then Becky asks, 'And what do you believe?'

'I believe I should be able to go out with who I want,' he's gazing right at her now, 'and marry who I want.' He turns away. 'But what kind of life is that for you, always having to meet like this. I can't even go to your mum's book-signing.'

She starts a little as he says this. It's funny how that book-signing has come to represent something. She's realising just what she's taking on, going out with him. This is where she'll start slipping away from him. How can he blame her? He gazes gloomily ahead of him. Now he doesn't feel angry so much as drained.

She gets up, looks at him for a moment, then says slowly, 'I guess lots of people meet in secret.' She gives a tiny smile. 'In a way I'll be just like all those women who see married men. I'll be like Andrea.'

'Andrea?'

'This woman my Dad was seeing secretly – for years it turns out – without my mum ever knowing.' And Becky thinks Andrea hung on there until Dad got a divorce. 'She really fought for my dad, unlike Mum, who just seemed to give up. But perhaps that's what you do if you find someone special. You've got to be strong-minded. And I've got to be just as strong-minded. Besides, it won't be for that long,' she says. 'I'm seventeen already and you're seventeen in a couple of weeks.'

He's standing up now. 'And when I'm eighteen,' he says, 'I can get a divorce from my family. And then I'll make it up to you – how I'll make it up to you.' Suddenly it all seems like a great adventure again.

'Just let them try and break us up,' cries Becky, 'just let them try.'

'We meet at last,' Becky's mum puts down her glass of wine. She's sitting behind a desk containing an ominously high pile of books and a large card which proclaims in fat capitals LOCAL AUTHOR.

Becky cannot bear to watch her mother now. Yet she cannot look at Adam either, who is standing on her right.

'Becky only told me about you last night,' she continues. 'Why are mothers always the last to be told about boyfriends?' she smiles across at Adam's mum who is keeping vigil over the cash till next to her. They exchange polite smiles, then Becky's mum says, 'But I sort of guessed anyhow, for Becky's been so amazingly quiet lately. I thought, either she's getting flu or she's met someone special,' she stretches out her hand, 'It's good to meet you, Mark.'

Mark springs forward from Becky's left side. And Becky watches them shake hands with such a sick feeling in her stomach. Deceiving her mum feels even worse than she'd expected. But there seemed no other way for Adam to be here without arousing his Mum's suspicion. Becky stares at Mrs Rosen's dark brown eyes. No, they wouldn't miss much.

'So why did you come to this book-signing – you've never been to a book-signing before?' Becky could hear all the questions she'd ask Adam. At least this way they've thrown her right off the scent.

Why shouldn't Adam accompany his best mate and his best mate's girlfriend.

Then she hears Mark say, 'I'd like to introduce you to my mate – well, our mate,' he laughs nervously, 'who really wanted to meet you.'

'You haven't said what his name is,' hisses Becky.

'Oh, he's called Adam,' says Mark with another nervous laugh.

Now Adam and her mum shake hands. In years to come they will laugh about this. Perhaps Mum will even shape it into a little story. 'And that was how I met my future son-in-law.'

Adam picks up a copy of *A Single Deception*.

'Er, would you mind signing it for me?' Becky hadn't expected him to do that. Her mum seems rather surprised, too.

'Now don't be all chivalrous and feel you have to buy it,' she says. 'It's fearsomely expensive, twelve pounds, ninety five.'

'No, I'd like it. I've never had a book signed before.' And I'm so desperate to make a good impression, Adam thinks. I want you to remember me.

'Well, aren't you wonderful,' cries Becky's mum.

She's got a long, pale face, surrounded on all sides by a mass of blonde curls, which sit on her head rather like a tea-cosy.

Her voice is lower than Becky's but with something of the same singsong quality. Both their voices rise up and down like perfectly tuned door bells.

She picks up a gold pen – and Becky whispers, 'Sign slowly, Mum, and you'll get more people over.' A small knot of people are watching them.

'It must be great signing a book you've written,' says Adam.

She puts her gold pen down. 'Writing a book, Adam, is like pulling yourself up a cliff by your fingernails. And some days, most days, you seem to do nothing but keep falling back down again. But when you finally reach the summit – there's no feeling quite like it.' They're really flashing the smiles back and forth now. She likes me, thinks Adam, triumphantly. He certainly likes her.

The owner of the shop, a large, jolly-looking woman, now appears brandishing a bottle of wine.

'More wine, Margaret?'

'Well, I shouldn't. So I will.'

Adam hands the book and three five pound notes over to his Mum.

'It's nice to see you taking an interest in books at last.'

He just knew she'd have to make some crack like that. It's funny, last night he'd felt really guilty about doing this. It was one thing to hide things from her – well, everyone does that. Didn't Jason say, 'If our parents knew the truth about any of us

133

they'd chuck us out of the house right away.' But deliberately lying to them – well, that made him uneasy. But now he thinks it serves her right. He's sick of her watching him and commenting on every little thing he does. He can't even buy a book without her writing a thesis about it. She hands him his change.

'I didn't know Mark had a girlfriend,' she murmurs. 'You never told me.'

Adam doesn't answer this. 'She seems very nice.' Actually she's bloody wonderful, Adam's so tempted to say something like that to her. One day he will.

Becky's mum is looking all around her. So is Becky, anxiously searching the horizon for more customers. Mark watches them, then says, 'Would you sign a copy for me too?'

'Certainly, but Mark don't feel you have to.'

'No, I'd like one, honestly,' says Mark.

Becky's mum picks up her gold pen, 'Well, I'll tell you what Mark, you'll have to come round for dinner soon.'

She likes him, thinks Mark. But then he thought she would. Mothers usually do, in fact they're often keener on him than their daughters are. He grins at her, then at Becky. Then he laughs at himself. For a second or two there, he really thought he was Becky's boyfriend. He was, what you might call, really getting into his role.

He didn't think he would. And when Becky first asked him to appear in this charade he said, 'No way.' He was amazed she even asked him. But then she kept on and on, practically begging him and finally she said how she couldn't ask anyone else as it would only be convincing with him.

That's when he knew he'd end up doing it. In a way he feels like Adam's understudy anyway. Now at least he's centre stage, playing the part he's always wanted. All right, it's only for half an hour, but then how long do most dreams last – a few seconds if you're lucky.

He spent a lot of time this morning deciding what to wear and in the end he decided on his smartest jacket and trousers. The first time you meet your girlfriend's parents you dress up a bit, don't you. That's why he's buying the book, too. It wouldn't look right if Becky's boyfriend didn't buy a copy.

'That's twelve pounds, ninety five,' says Adam's mum.

'A bargain,' says Mark. 'This signed book will be selling at Sotheby's one day, I'm sure – not that I'll ever sell it.' He's really flirting with Becky's mum now. She'll be inviting him to come and move in next. He dives into his pocket, pulls out a five pound note and three coins, then digs around for the other note. It's not there. It must be. His digging becomes decidedly frantic now. Then finally

135

he hisses, 'Becky, you couldn't lend us a fiver could you.' Then to Becky's mum he says, 'Left all my other money in my other jacket. Don't like to carry too much money around – you know, pick-pockets and all that.'

Becky hands him the five pound note and immediately he says 'I'll pay you back first thing, Monday – before nine o'clock you'll have your money back.' He turns to Becky's mum. 'Got my other suit loaded with cash.'

Becky squeezes his hand. She doesn't care about the money. She owes him a lot more than money for today. Then suddenly Adam catches her eye. It's the first time he's dared do that since they arrived. How absurd this all is. But at least he's here, smuggled in past the enemy.

Suddenly, he winks at her. She winks back.

Then she looks at Mrs Rosen and thinks, *if you knew*. But you don't. Today we have scored a small, but important, victory. The first of many.

# 6 One of Mark's Better Days, and Lauren's Worst

Mark washes the toothpaste off his neck. Where had he heard that toothpaste would reduce it? Anyway it doesn't. It seems there's nothing he can do. He is doomed to carry aound the biggest, ugliest lovebite the world's ever seen.

As soon as he came home last night his mum was homing in on it. 'What happened to you?' she demanded.

He explains. 'I had a small accident on my neck.' His dad, of course, thought it was hilarious. 'Been attacked by a hoover, have you, son?' And even after he went to bed, Mark could still hear his Dad rumbling away with laughter.

Mark, the joke as usual. He slinks back to his bedroom. He'll have to wear his polo-neck today and for the next couple of weeks. Not that suddenly wearing a polo-neck isn't a dead giveaway. And then they'll all sit round cracking jokes. What was he doing messing about with Pam the vampire anyhow. Last night he'd just gone out for a quiet drink with Jason and a couple of Jason's mates. And then this girl, known to all as Pam the vampire, slimed over and started stroking his knee. Only she was sending Mark up, he realised that all right. So just to show her what she was dealing with Mark suddenly leaned over and gave her this massive french kiss. Then, he was outside with her. And all at once she started ripping away at his neck. And it was so painful. It still aches a bit, actually.

He digs out a white polo-neck he hasn't worn for centuries and glares at his trainers, they certainly haven't brought him much luck. Then he stumbles donwstairs. As always, a smell of burnt toast wafts over the kitchen. Today the smell makes him heave. He feels dreadful. He slumps down at the kitchen table. He can't see his mum too well but he senses she isn't looking any too friendly.

'Look at you,' she says. 'Well, I just hope your weekend was worth it.'

It wasn't. This is what makes this scene so undeniably tragic. And yet it had begun so amazingly well, with him posing as Becky's boyfriend. It was certainly his most convincing acting performance to date. And if a talent scout from Hollywood had observed him he'd surely have been snapped up for a five year contract now. But instead, Becky disappeared with Adam and he was left with a huge nothingness inside him.

'You know I don't like you going out before a college day,' his mum says. 'I certainly didn't see you do much homework over the weekend.'

'Look, just let me get my head together, will you, Mum. Then you can nag me all you like.'

She sniffs and disappears. Then she returns with a large pot of coffee.

'Toast?' she asks. Mark closes his eyes.

'No thanks.'

'Cereal?'

He groans.

Now she's peering under Mark's polo-neck.

'Mum, please.'

She shakes her head. 'You know you can get an infection from those things, don't you?'

'No, I didn't, Mum, but thanks for letting me know. I can't tell you how much you've cheered me up.'

Still, Mark thinks, he feels so bad now nothing can make him feel any worse. But an hour later he is plumbing new depths of despair. He is sitting in the sports shop office with Jason learning what he did last night.

Jason tells him, 'You kept saying "I've got to get a woman of my own. I've got to get a woman of my own." '

'How loudly?'

139

Jason hesitates.

'Tell me. I can take it.'

'Well, pretty loudly.'

'And then?'

'Then you went over to those girls who said they came from London, and you sang to them.'

'I remember,' says Mark. 'But that was all right, wasn't it. I mean I haven't got a bad voice, have I?'

'No, your voice was great – very clear. It was your choice of song.'

'What did I sing?' Mark leans forward. 'Come on, tell me, Jason.'

' "Like a Virgin." '

'I didn't!' Mark exclaims. 'Oh, I'm leaving town tonight. I'm out of here.' He closes his eyes. 'What did I do then?'

'Then you went off with Pam the vampire,' he grins, 'and got your tattoo. Then you . . .'

'No, don't tell me any more.' Mark puts his hands over his face. 'I bet it'll be all round the college what a toerag I made of myself last night.'

'Nah, everyone just thought you were out of your head.'

'But that's just it,' cries Mark. 'I wasn't, I mean I only had one half of lager all evening and even I can't get drunk on that. It wasn't alcohol that did it – it was women.'

He sighs dramatically, 'Man, I've got to get a woman of my own. I'm desperate. Yet last night,

140

apart from Pam the vampire, no girl looked at me twice. Why, what did I do wrong? Come on Jason, tell me, I need guidance, mate.'

Jason gets up and slowly paces back and forth, his eyes half closed. How often had Mark seen him walk up and down the hut as he worked out what they should do next. He said he always thought better on his feet.

'All right, Markie,' says Jason. 'First of all you were too eager, and that always puts people off. You rushed at it. Like that girl with the red hair who smiled at you – remember her?'

Marks nods.

'And do you remember what you said to her?'

'Not exactly.'

'You charged up to her exclaiming, ' "Hiya babe, I'm a rocking hormone." '

Mark starts to groan again.

'But don't worry,' says Jason. 'We all make mistakes. Even me. Very occasionally. Anyway, here's Jason's guide to women. The golden rule is you've got to play it cool, assess what kind of girl you're dealing with, suss her out. You see, everyone's got an angle on things and you've got to find out what her angle is. Then you can work out how to get her to like you. And when she likes you – that's when you play hard to get.'

The door opens. Tania hisses, 'The boss's car is just pulling up.'

141

'Cheers, Tania, make it look as if we've started the stocktaking, will you? I'll be right there.' She smiles and disappears.

'I thought I might get some new clothes too. Give myself a different image,' says Mark. 'Maybe even get a suit like yours with wide shoulders. I've saved a bit from my job.' From time to time Mark works at the local newsagent.

'Don't go for a suit that's too trendy – it'll be out of fashion after you've worn it a couple of times. And whatever you do, don't get clip on braces, they are really tacky, get button-on braces.'

'Button-on braces,' repeats Mark.

'And if you need a loan,' says Jason.

'No, I'm okay – actually if you could lend me a fiver until Saturday . . . I owe Becky . . .'

'No prob,' says Jason. 'I get pretty good wages now for a shop worker.' He hands him ten pounds. 'No rush about paying me back. And remember what I told you, play it cool, play hard to get.'

Mark nods, 'It's just it's difficult playing hard to get when you want a woman so desperately. It's only when I get a proper girlfriend I'll be able to . . . I just can't get her out of my head.' A look of real sympathy suddenly passes between them. Jason's pacing furiously now. He says, 'Sometimes a girl gets into your bloodstream. And there's nothing you can do about it. You just go on carrying her about wherever you go.'

142

'Mark, you could always go to the chemist. I'm sure they would give you something.' Becky stares anxiously across at Mark. It is lunchtime and they are sitting in a packed college refectory. They don't normally eat here but Mark said he didn't feel like walking into town today. He isn't in a good mood.

'I'm not going to the chemist about a lovebite,' he snaps.

'No, okay, perhaps if I go in and ask how about that?' Becky can't help feeling responsible somehow for the eyesore on Mark's neck. What's worse, Mark keeps giving her these evil glares as if he thinks it's her fault.

She should never have asked him to be her boyfriend, not when he had this crush on her. But after the three of them left the book-signing on Saturday she was almost pleading with Mark to join Adam and her for a coffee. She'd known that if he went off on his own he'd only get all depressed. She knew it. But he just kept saying, 'Thanks but I've got things to do.' He was really stubborn about it.

Dare she ask him to be her boyfriend just once more. She'd talked and talked with Adam about it last night and they both decided the only way she could safely attend Adam's birthday party next week would be with Mark on her arm. But how she dreads asking him. Yet what else can she do? It's all Adam's parents' fault. They're the ones

Mark should be frowning at. Not her. Oh, what a mess it all is.

Then she gives a little exclamation of irritation. The guy behind her keeps moving his chair back on to hers. She won't have room to breathe soon.

'Excuse me,' she calls, 'but do you mind moving your chair back a bit.' There's no response. She calls again, louder this time. 'Excuse me, but will you move back a bit. You're really squashing me here.' This does get a response; the guy thrusts his chair even further forward.

'Do you mind,' gasps Becky. Then Mark calls, 'Come on, you heard the lady, move your chair back now.' The guy waves his two fingers in the air which causes a loud cackle of laughter from the other blokes on his table.

'Move your chair back,' growls Mark. 'The lady's asked you twice and she won't ask you a third time.'

This time the guy turns round. And Mark stares at him in horror and amazement. Of all the people it could be – it's him – Ian Saltmore, one of the leaders of that gang who beat him up on the way home from school, all those years ago. Mark can feel his heart hammering as the nightmare spins round in his head once more.

It's strange. Most memories are just like sudden bursts of light. They flash in and out of your head for a second or two and then they've gone again.

144

Even the best times are often little more than frag-
ments now. But Mark can remember every detail
of that afternoon. He can replay the whole scene
and even freeze-frame the worst parts, like the
moment when he cowered and cringed and
squeaked for mercy like a terrified nannygoat, while
Ian Saltmore's smile grew larger and larger.

Ian Saltmore's smiling now, 'You talking to me?'
he says.

'Yes,' cries Mark. 'Move your chair, now, dog-
breath.'

There're excited exclamations of laughter and
cries of 'Did you hear what he called you, Ian,'
from Saltmore's table, while Becky whispers across
to Mark, 'Leave it, Mark, it's not important.' But
Saltmore is already hoisting his beer-belly out of
his chair and lumbering over to Mark.

Mark, shaking only very slightly, gets up too.

'I want an apology,' says Saltmore, his tone even
and relaxed. This is a mere formality, just to keep
up his reputation in the canteen. Mark clearly isn't
worth getting into a lather about.

'Leave it, please,' says Becky.

But Mark doesn't appear to hear. Instead he
solemnly takes off his glasses and hands them to
Becky. He can see much better without them.
Becky stares at the glasses in astonishment.

'What are you doing Mark – he's twice your
size.'

145

Saltmore can't resist a little snigger as Mark squares up to him.

'I want an apology, squirt,' he says.

'I don't give a flying toss what you want,' cries Mark.

Saltmore squints down at him. Mark can almost hear him asking himself who is this guy and why is he acting like this to me.

The next moment Saltmore's considerably more astonished, though, for a fist suddenly comes flying towards his chin. A fist with all Mark's energy behind it. He wants to split Saltmore's face open, at least. He doesn't achieve this. In truth, he barely grazes Saltmore's chin. But Saltmore certainly isn't smiling any more and his face is turning very, very red.

Not that Mark has long to enjoy this burst of technicolor. For Saltmore's fist comes thundering towards him and scores a direct hit on his jaw. For a second Mark is triumphant. Saltmore really let go at him that time. He's got to him at last. But then all he can think about is the pain. It's excruciating. It's as if his face has just collided with a metal pole.

And then he hears Saltmore roar, 'Say you're sorry,' and Becky who's right beside him is crying, 'Yes, he's sorry.' But then Mark fishes up a scrap of voice and gargles rather than says, 'No, no, never.' Immediately there's another even more powerful explosion on his face. Only this time the pain seems to be above him too, pressing down on his head. Mark sways backwards. Don't pass out. Inside his head he's yelling the words at himself. Don't pass out.

But the back of Saltmore's hand is hurtling towards him for a third assault. Only this time it gets intercepted. Becky has snatched hold of Saltmore's fist and is screaming, 'Leave him alone, you big bully.' Saltmore swears at her but he steps back. And then a dinner lady appears, tiny and elderly, like a battered wren, declaring, 'If you don't stop now I'm calling the principal and he'll have you all suspended.'

'It's his fault,' cries Becky pointing at Saltmore. Some of the crowd gathered round murmur their agreement. Saltmore turns to his mates. 'I only asked him to say he's sorry.' Then he yells at Mark. 'Just what is your problem?' There's no answer at first then Mark splutters, 'I'm not sorry,' blood trickling out of his mouth as he speaks.

The right side of his face has gone all numb now while the rest of him feels oddly weightless. In fact, he wouldn't be too surprised if at any moment he started floating upwards.

He closes his eyes for a second, then he hears Becky say, 'Here, take this, Mark.' It's a handkerchief which he presses up to his nose. 'We're just going up the corridor to the loo, all right.' He's

147

not sure if he can make it. But then Becky puts her arm around him and he starts walking as firmly as he can. He keeps closing his eyes and even when he's got them open everything looks distinctly hazy.

Then he smells a familiar perfume and hears a familiar voice, cry, 'Oh, no, what's happened?' Lauren swims before him.

'Mark got into a fight in the canteen,' says Becky. 'I'm still not sure why,' she adds.

'How are you feeling, Mark?' Lauren asks, putting an arm round his other side.

'I've felt better,' he mutters, his voice now distinctly nasal.

When Mark looks up again he sees they're heading for the ladies. 'I'm not going in there,' he mumbles.

'Oh, but Mark, we've got to . . .' begins Becky.

'It's all right,' says Lauren. 'We'll take him in the men's.'

As they go inside Lauren declares, 'Why do men's toilets always smell so much worse then women's.' The one guy who's in the loo washing his hands looks up guiltily and then bolts for the door.

'Lots of cold water, Becky,' says Lauren. 'I'll get Mark a chair.'

Becky switches on the taps and is just pressing the handkerchief on to Mark's face, when Lauren returns with a chair.

'Sit down here Mark,' she says. He slumps gratefully on to the chair.

'Now put your head back,' says Becky.

'Actually,' says Lauren, 'there's no need for Mark to hold his head back. It's probably better for him to sit up.'

Becky lets Mark sit forward.

The toilet door opens. 'Get out,' says Lauren, without even looking round. 'There's someone ill in here.' The door slams shut again. Becky can't help admiring Lauren's assurance, even while being slightly irritated by it.

Mark looks up at Becky, bending over him. If he had a bit more energy he could feel feel quite sexy now. Then she and Lauren swop round. 'Wish it would stop bleeding,' he mumbles.

'It will, Mark, don't worry,' says Lauren. But it's another five minutes before the bleeding finally stops. Even sitting down, Mark feels quite giddy. Then he suddenly thinks of something.

'I haven't lost any teeth, have I, Lauren?'

'Just the two front ones.'

'Oh, what!'

Lauren smiles, 'Only joking.' He heaves a sigh of relief, then gazes down at his poloneck. Blood is splattered all over it. He won't be able to wear it tomorrow, and it's the only poloneck he's got. So how can he cover up the eyesore on his neck? Lauren follows his gaze and his thoughts, then

gives her hearty laugh. She was the first to sight
the lovebite this morning. Mark can't help laughing, too.

'Everyone knows about it anyway,' he says.

'I guessed as soon as I saw that musty old
poloneck,' says Lauren. She turns to Becky who is
leaning against the sink. 'You all right?' she asks.

'Yes, fine, Lauren,' says Becky. 'Just wasn't
expecting all this.'

'Now, tell me. What exactly happened?'

Becky begins to explain. 'This lager lout sitting
behind me kept pushing his chair back on to mine.
I asked him politely to move . . .'

'It was Ian Saltmore,' interrupts Mark. Lauren
immediately lets out a low gasp. Becky watches
them curiously; it's as if that name's a secret pass-
word or something.

'Who's Ian Saltmore?' asks Becky. But neither
Lauren nor Mark seem to hear her. Suddenly
they're locked together, as Mark exclaims, 'I stood
up to him, this time, Lauren.'

'Last time was nothing to be ashamed of,' says
Lauren. She's kneeling beside him. 'It was twenty
to one.'

'I humiliated myself, Lauren. There's no denying it,' and in his mind's eye that scene unspools
yet again. There he is begging for mercy and there
– suddenly the scene seems to jump. And there is
Mark, in the canteen, standing up to Saltmore,

150

refusing to give in. 'But today, I regained my honour.'

'Regained your honour,' murmurs Lauren. 'You've been spending too much time with Jason. Fighting never solves anything.' But her arm is round him too.

'Ian Saltmore was one of the gang you told me about,' says Becky. They look up at her as if they'd forgotten she was there.

'Ian Saltmore, attacked you after school,' continues Becky. She's talking very slowly, as if she's speaking in an unfamiliar language.

'That's right,' says Mark. 'And Becky was brilliant, Lauren. That guy was going to punch me a third time when she yanked hold of his hand and started mouthing away at him.'

Becky kneels down too. 'I didn't know what I was saying. And weren't his hands just huge. I mean my hands just got lost in them. Biggest hands I've seen.'

Lauren's smiling at her now. And Mark, his face still streaked with blood, is positively beaming at her as he declares, 'This is turning into one of my better days'.

The lesson Lauren dreads being late for is History, as Mrs Allen sticks her arm out in front of you and leaves it there like a banner while she lectures you about time-keeping. Still, at least Lauren's got a good excuse this time.

She opens the classroom door, then groans inwardly. Mrs Allen isn't taking the class, Grant is. She just can't seem to escape him these days. She'll be sitting in the refectory and suddenly, there he'll be. And he just stands there, pretending to look around, but really he's watching her. Sometimes she'll glance up and catch his eye. Then he'll deliberately look away again. But an hour later in the library or somewhere, up he'll pop again. He seems just to spring out of nowhere. This must be a coincidence though. He wouldn't cover a lesson just because of her.

As she goes to sit down there's a definite buzz of interest from the class. Most of the college clearly think there's a steamy love affair going on between Grant and her. And at first it amused her to let them think that. At first!

'I'm sorry I'm late,' she says, 'but Mark was, er taken ill.'

'Nothing serious, I hope,' says Grant.

'No, he's all right, but Becky's had to take him home.' Actually Becky's taken him to her house, as Mark didn't want his mum to see him looking, as he puts it, so bloody.

'You will no doubt have noticed that I am not Mrs Allen,' says Grant. This is how Lauren likes him to talk to her in class, just as if she's an ordinary student. She relaxes a little. 'Mrs Allen has flu and I am her humble understudy.' He stretches his arms out to the class. 'Is there no end to this man's talents, you ask yourself.' He stares around for a reaction. For all his air of superiority Grant likes laughter, applause, fuss. Lauren watches his eyes shine when he stirs the class into laughter. So it must be all the more disheartening when the applause dries up, which it has since the rumours about Lauren and him started spreading.

And he doesn't, as Lauren expected, perform for the whole lesson. Instead, he writes some questions for them on the board and sits staring into a textbook. Lauren only looks up when she hears the girls behind her giggling and then she sees Grant isn't looking at his text book any longer.

He's staring right at her, as if there's no one else in the room. Only his eyes are suddenly wide and very sad. She shivers without quite knowing why. What's he looking at her like that for?

Recently she's tried gently to put him off. She hasn't been available on the days he's suggested and she's hoped things would just drift off, without her having to say anything. But that doesn't seem to be happening. Right now, Lauren wants to see as little of Grant as possible.

As soon as the class finishes Lauren is the first out of the door. And she practically runs to the library. Seated at one of the desks there are three

153

girls from her English group. They see her and look up quizzically, then start whispering and giggling. Lauren sweeps past them. Then she gets out her English homework. She's got three As in a row now which is quite exceptional. But she's worked for each result. She looks across at the girls and she hopes they've noticed how hard she's working on the English project; this is a study of an author you admire. Lauren chose Katherine Mansfield, partly because she admired her stories, but partly because her life was so tragic, all those years of ill health and dying at just thirty-four. That really gave Lauren a jolt. If Lauren died that young that would mean she'd had half her life already.

Once, years ago, Cathy had asked her what she'd do if she only had one hour left to live. And Lauren had given a wicked laugh and said she'd chase over to Jason's house . . . but that was long before she ever went out with him.

Lauren puts the lid on those memories and spends time browsing in the nineteenth century literature section, gathering up additional information about Katherine Mansfield. Then she returns to her desk, picks up her bag and walks up to the library exit. She is miles away, still thinking about Katherine Mansfield's life, when the alarm bell suddenly shrieks into life. Lauren springs back as if she's been bitten. A librarian is standing beside her, the one with severely-cut grey hair who'd once

154

asked a student if he could yawn more quietly. Lauren turns to her. 'Why did it do that?' asks Lauren.

Lauren can see the librarian sizing her up, before saying, 'It's been playing up recently.'

'It gave me the shock of my life,' says Lauren. 'I expected fifteen policemen to appear,' but even as she says this, she notices a tallish man stepping out of the library office.

'Try putting your bag through again,' says the librarian. As Lauren edges through the barrier, the alarm starts again, if anything even louder than before. Lauren turns round. 'Something's wrong with the machine,' she announces calmly, but inside she's shaking. The librarian says, 'May I check your bag please?' and her hand is on the bag before Lauren can reply. The librarian puts the bag onto the nearest desk and starts emptying it, while that man is standing right beside the barrier now. Perhaps there's another man standing outside shouting into a walkie-talkie, 'Warning, warning, book thief about to make a dash for it.'

It's comic really, but Lauren can't raise the tiniest smile. Instead she's asking herself – I didn't put one of those Katherine Mansfield books in by mistake, did I? But no, how could she have – she never brought any of the books over to her desk. She's innocent. There's nothing to worry about.

And then out of Lauren's bag is hauled a book she doesn't recognise.

'Is this a library book?' asks the librarian staring intently at her. It's called *A Guide to Twentieth Century Literature* and on the side it's got one of those labels all the library books have. 'Yes, I think it is,' says Lauren, 'but I didn't put it there.' Then the librarian pulls out another book, *English Literature 1870 – 1970*. There's a horrible sick feeling in Lauren's mouth as she says, 'I didn't put that book in there either.'

'And you don't know how these books got in your bag?' says the librarian, her voice almost eerily calm. But then this probably happens a lot. And everyone, no doubt, gives the same excuse. Only in Lauren's case it is the truth. But how can she make anyone believe that.

'Who do you think put the books in your bag then?'

'I don't know,' says Lauren. But she can hazard a very good guess.

'Well, I think it's best we discuss the matter in the office, don't you,' says the librarian, her manner still icily polite.

Inside the office the librarian sits down. In the middle of the desk is a thin plastic lunch box containing sandwiches and an apple, while beside it is a flask. They don't seem the right props for what's happening now.

The librarian writes down Lauren's name and address and her college tutor's name and what A Levels she's doing. When she says, English, the librarian's head bobs up. She doesn't say anything but Lauren can sense the case against her is growing. Then the librarian says,

'And you still don't know how the books got in your bag?'

'No, I just know I didn't put them in there.'

'But you can't tell me who did?'

Lauren is almost tempted to name the three girls from her English group. It must be them. Who else would bother. And they knew exactly what books would look most incriminating. But she can't sneak. Apart from the fact it's unethical, it'd only make everyone in the college hate her even more.

If only Cathy were here. Normally Cathy would be. It's just today she's gone for an interview at The Record Room. But she said she'd be back by now. Why is she letting me down? I'm being silly. It's not Cathy's fault. It's just I need her here so badly – her and Jason. Why does she want Jason here? Cathy always says Jason is good in emergencies. So that must be why – well partly.

Lauren's thinking about Jason so hard that when there's a knock at the door she whirls round, half-expecting . . . but it's a lecturer asking about exam papers and the librarian talks in whispers to him at the doorway, and then she must have said something about Lauren for the lecturer gives her such a disapproving glance that Lauren thinks she'll explode with anger and guilt. That's the awful thing, she hasn't done anything but she feels guilty.

And when the librarian says, 'We take a very serious view of this. A letter will be sent to your parents,' Lauren starts blushing with shame.

The office door finally opens. She is released but with sentence still to be passed. The librarian clearly expects her to flee. But instead, Lauren just charges down towards the library. Where are they? But of course the three girls have gone.

Not that they have flown very far. They're sitting on the steps leading out of reception, squawking and laughing. They look like starlings, Lauren thinks.

She glares down at these starlings in human form, unable to speak at first, she's so angry. Then she bursts out, 'Why did you put those books in my bag?' Anna, their leader, gives her a languid glance.

'Don't know what you're talking about.' She is totally unconvincing and Lauren rather suspects that she knows it.

'I want you to come to the library with me now and tell them what you did.' Lauren's voice sounds horribly shrill.

'Us, why should we?' they cry almost in unison. Their smugness makes Lauren's eyes water.

158

'Well, I hope you are proud of yourselves,' she cries. 'I think you're pathetic.' She'd say more only she senses they're enjoying all this.

She pushes her way through them and down the steps. Then she calls up,

'You haven't heard the last of this. I'm going to make you very sorry for what you've done.'

Suddenly she has their full attention. They're all staring at her now or rather they're staring at someone who is standing just inches away from her – Grant.

'May I have a word, Lauren?' he murmurs. He is the last person she wants to talk to now. But before she can reply he is already walking over to the chairs in reception. But then Anna says in a piercingly loud whisper, 'I'm not doing any English homework any more. I'm having a sordid affair instead.'

Lauren expects Grant to pretend not to hear this. Just as in class when he ignores all the sound effects which accompany her every time she gets an A. But this time he springs round. 'What did you say?'

Anna clearly wasn't expecting this and Lauren drinks in her discomfort. 'I wasn't talking to you,' cries Grant. 'And I'll kick you out of my class if I hear that kind of comment again, do you understand?'

Anna gapes at him in shocked bewilderment.

Never has Grant spoken to a student like that before.

'And get up,' he yelps. 'No one can walk past you draped over the steps like that.' Grant must have stepped across students sitting on the steps a hundred times this term, without making any comment at all. The girls, clearly still shocked, slowly pick up their bags.

'Now go on, move, you're making this place untidy.' Grant suddenly turns round and looks at Lauren as if she's an accomplice or something. The girls must have seen this too, for as they slink past they flash Lauren a look of such undiluted hatred, it's like a fist flying into her face. She gazes at them, stunned, incredulous, furious. Why do they hate her so much? Grant's outburst was nothing to do with her. Well, in a way, it was. But what's important is that she's only seen him three times. She hasn't even kissed him. Why won't anyone believe that? Why won't even Grant believe that?

All at once she can take no more, and she's racing out of reception, out of the college grounds . . . and then just carries on running. She hasn't run this fast since she fled from her fifteenth birthday party. Then she was running away from Jason. Now, without quite knowing why, she's racing towards him.

160

Jason is leaving for a late lunchbreak. But first he picks up a large envelope and puts it under his arm. It is empty but that doesn't matter, it makes him look purposeful. As he glide-struts around the town he sees Tania standing at the top of the steps leading up to the bus shelter. He springs up the steps and Tania flushes guiltily. She was due back fifteen minutes ago. She is talking to two girls.

'Hello, Tania', says Jason. 'Introduce me to your friends then.' But before Tania can reply the taller of the two girls is saying,

'Hello, I'm Michelle.'

'Michelle, that's a very sexy name,' he grins cheekily as Michelle blushes. Then Jason checks out her pupils. They're expanding wildly, of course. It's amazing how easy it is to flirt with girls you don't particularly fancy.

'And I'm Marie,' says the other girl impatiently.

'Marie,' Jason repeats the name as if it were a magic spell, then adds, 'You're going out with Paul Miller, aren't you?'

'How do you know that?' she asks.

Jason knew that because Paul Miller had been in his shop on Saturday going on and on about his new girlfriend. But Jason never reveals his sources.

'I am the knower of all things,' he says.

'And you're Jason, aren't you,' asks Marie.

'I claim that honour, yes.' Then both girls peer at Tania and giggle, while Tania just looks mighty embarrassed. Clearly Tania has been talking to them about Jason. Marie says, 'We'll leave you two alone then,' but before she leaves she nudges Tania and whispers.

'You're right, Tania, he's dead horny.'

'Those two,' says Tania. 'They're about as subtle as a brick.' Even her two spots have turned bright red.

'What have you been saying about me then?' asks Jason lightly.

'I think you're big-headed enough already,' replies Tania.

'Oh, go on,' says Jason. 'I can stand it.'

Tania just smiles, but then says suddenly. 'By the way Jason, when are you going to ask me out?'

This catches him by surprise. He stares at her, long blonde hair, very appealing face, nice legs and she's got a warm personality too. She's very nearly the girl of his dreams. The trouble is she looks too much like someone else and every time he went out with her he knew who he'd be thinking about. And he likes Tania too much to use her. But rejection is something that has to be handled very, very carefully. Whenever you turn a girl down you've got to make sure you've left her with some dignity, some self-respect. And if you can, always leave her smiling. This is what Jason is aiming for now.

'The way I see it, Tania,' he says, 'you've got to think of our children. I mean, just think what they would look like. They'd be so amazingly beautiful and so incredibly hunky, that they'd never get a moment's peace, they'd be mobbed wherever they went . . .' He sees her give a little shiver as if she's just received a small electric shock. He can feel the sting himself. He changes gear.

'And besides, Tania, you're far too good for me.'

She looks up. 'I can be mean.'

'Not as mean as me. No one's as mean as me.'

She smiles, then tears form in the corners of her eyes. She fumbles for a handkerchief, then sees Jason flourishing one in front of her. She laughs, 'You,' she shakes her head. Then she asks, 'Who is she, then?'

'Who?'

'The girl who stole your heart away.'

Jason backs away slightly. 'You've been overdosing on *The Waltons* again.'

Tania puts her handkerchief away. 'No, come on, I know there's someone. Who is she?' Jason starts tapping his envelope. She makes it all sound so cosy and sweet and about as dangerous as a pint of lucozade. Whereas, really meeting someone special is like, it's like standing on the edge of a railway platform: quiet, calm, peaceful. And then suddenly, from out of nowhere, comes this great monster hurtling past you at such a speed, you can't see or hear anything else. You are completely overpowered. And, finally, you fall off the platform

and down, way down into . . . Lauren's fifteenth
birthday party.

Walking into her party, with a girl on his arm,
was just a test, that's all. He had to know what
Lauren really felt for him. Yet, short of putting a
video camera inside her head, how could he ever
know. In the end, he became so crazed, that this
test seemed like the only solution. But as soon as
he saw Lauren's face, he knew he'd caused a wreck
of epic proportions.

There were no survivors.

He stands there clenching the envelope so tightly
his knuckles turn white.

'What?' Then he sees where she's pointing.
'Yeah, that's Lauren.'

'Anyway, I'd better go.'

'Right, see you later.'

As she disappears he steps forward, 'Lauren.'
Lauren looks up and up. So there he is. He seems
just to spring out of the scene around him, like a
cut-out. He's smiling and beckoning her up, then
immediately starts bounding down towards her.
They meet on the platform in the middle.

Lauren stares at him, unexpectedly, absurdly
shy. 'Heard about Mark?' she asks.

'Yeah, he rang. Brilliant, isn't it?' His dark eyes
glitter. 'Cathy was in my shop a short while ago.
She got that job at The Record Room.'

'Oh, great.'

164

He moves closer to her. 'You all right?'

'Yes, why?'

'You look a bit breathless, if you know what I mean.'

And yes, there it is, the smile that has snared so many. The smile that snared her long ago.

'Actually, Jason, something rather nasty just happened.' Then she tells him about the library, the words just tumbling out. His face remains masklike but she can feel him tensing up.

'Know who did it?' he asks. 'Give me their names and addresses and they won't have any windows left tonight.'

Lauren feels a ripple of excitement. He'd do it as well. She could see him charging off to battle, her white knight. Then he'd return to her, eager for the next daring deed.

But no, this problem can't be solved like that. 'It wouldn't help,' she says sadly. 'There's a queue of people just waiting to hate me at the moment.'

'Why?' He looks astonished.

So far, she's studiously avoided mentioning Grant. But of course Jason knows all about him. He even had a fight in the sports shop defending her honour. There's no escaping Grant. It's incredible how three evenings can stretch into every corner of her life.

But Jason must know the truth. 'Well, there's this English lecturer, Grant,' the name seems to

165

echo around them. 'He took me out to the theatre and cinema – as friends.' This sounds rather weak. 'I mean, I always wanted to go to the cinema and theatre and he offered to take me.' Why does she feel so embarrassed explaining all this to Jason. He's not her boyfriend. 'There is absolutely nothing in it but you know how rumours start.'

Jason takes her hand and stares at her. He looks as if he's going to ask her to dance or something. And rignt now, Lauren wouldn't have cared if he had. He's smiling at her again now. And then Lauren hears a voice calling her. No, surely he can't have followed her here. She gazes down. It's Grant.

She stares guiltily. Grant is squinting up at her. He looks as if he might climb up towards her. And she doesn't want Jason to hear this conversation. She senses it's going to be embarrassing and mis-leading.

'Jason, I'll see you later,' she says.

He just nods grimly. But as she starts going down the steps he calls, 'Lauren.'

She looks up.

'If ever you need any immoral support, just call me.'

She smiles and lets her eyes rest on him for a moment, before trudging downwards.

'Are you all right?' asks Grant.

'Yes, fine,' she says briskly.

166

'I think we should have a coffee. I want to talk to you.'

'Sorry, I'm in a rush.'

'It is important.'

'Is it about my English?'

He starts at this, then says, 'No, it's about us.'

But there is no 'us'. There never was. He's twisting their three evenings into something they weren't. He's deceiving himself and everyone else. She wants to tell him that. But he's also her tutor and how do you tell your tutor he's misread a situation. She looks up for Jason. He's gone. She's disappointed but not surprised. Grant's making everything look so incriminating.

'You are keeping Friday week clear in your diary, aren't you?' says Grant. 'That's the night of the party.'

'The party,' echoes Lauren, dully. Then she remembers. There's a private party being held at Swanks, a new club just outside Cartford. It's going to be quite a big affair, apparently. Alex Goodwin, a local entrepreneur, is holding it and the guest list is a real who's who of local notables. Grant got an invite because he taught one of Alex Goodwin's daughters English last year. At the time it had sounded exciting, now all she sees is Grant staring intently at her.

What happened to the aloof, witty, superior Grant. That was the Grant she liked and felt safe

167

with. And she feels oddly cheated by this mushy impostor who keeps pushing her further into his world than she wants to go.

'How can you have forgotten about the party?' That fairly mocking tone has returned to his voice now but his tiny eyes are still boring into hers.

'I'll pick you up for the party at eight o'clock, the usual place.' His tone is crisp, factual, no nonsense. She's heard that tone in class when they dispute a date for homework. You will complete the homework on time; you will come out on a date with me. He leans forward and fumbles in his briefcase. 'Oh, yes, this is for you.' He looks awkward. He hands her a huge hardback book entitled, 'The Cinema of David Lynch.'

'As you enjoyed his new film so much, I thought you might appreciate this too.' And Lauren had enjoyed seeing the new David Lynch film with Grant and discussing it afterwards in that coffee bar. This, she thought, is what university will be like and she'd appreciated this taste of things to come.

She opens the book, looking first at the price – eighteen pounds, ninety five p, what a price for a book, and then the inscription: To Lauren, a bewitching and stimulating companion. G. She has to smile at the G. Isn't it a bit late for secrecy now? But still, it is generous of him, absurdly generous, in fact. And it's a thoughtful gift.

'Thanks for the book. I'll enjoy reading it,' she says gently. He leans forward. 'Now what about that coffee. I was so worried about you when you ran out of college . . .' Give him an inch and he'll run a marathon.

Lauren lowers her eyes. 'No, I must go. I really must. Goodbye.' She walks quickly away, praying Grant won't follow her. She plans to go to the sports shop and wait for Jason. But in the end she just gets the bus home.

Today is clearly one of those days when only nasty things happen. She closes her eyes. And she just feels so incredibly tired. Then she thinks of Jason calling after her to ask if she needed any immoral support. But not even Jason can help her out of this one.

What is she going to do about Grant? She's got to end this with Grant, once and for all. Yet she's not sure how to do it. To be honest, she feels totally out of her depth.

She peers outside the bus window. It's only half-past three but already it's getting dark. That dull, grey twilight, which is always more depressing than real darkness. A dismal nothingness. How many days without Jason have felt just like that.

Lauren wraps her arms round herself, although the bus is not cold.

Never has she felt more alone.

*

Cathy picks up the phone. 'Hello, Cathy speaking.'

'It's me.' Jason never deigns to say his name. He just assumes his voice is instantly recognisable, which it is.

'You've been out a lot.'

'Yeah, well we're planning an animal rights rally on . . .'

'I've rung you twice.'

'I know. I was just about to ring you. Honestly.'

His tone softens. 'I need your help. I know it's hard to believe.' He hesitates. 'Actually, it's about Lauren.' Cathy feels a surge of excitement. 'Oh, yes.'

'Is Lauren still seeing that mutant?'

'You mean Grant.'

'Yeah.'

'I think so,' says Cathy, gently. Actually she'd had a long talk with Lauren about Grant this morning. At Cathy's urging Lauren was to go and talk to him after English and finish it. Only Lauren's bag with all her homework in went missing. Somebody had put it in one of the French rooms. It took Lauren and Cathy over an hour to find it. And she was too worked up to talk to Grant after that. And then Lauren decided it would be easier to talk to Grant away from college and at Swanks. Then she would be on neutral territory, as it were. In a way, Cathy agrees with her. Yet she can't help wondering if Lauren isn't just putting off the inevitable.

170

'Where and when is she meeting this creep?' asks Jason. Cathy sits down on the chair by the phone. If she tells Jason, will she be interfering, sticking her nose in again. She thinks of Lauren and the truth game and shudders inwardly.

'Cathy, tell me.'

Cathy wants to tell him. But what if she does and everything goes wrong?

'Cathy, I watched Lauren in town a couple of days ago and secretly watched her with that guy and she's really unhappy with him.' There's just the tiniest crack in his voice. Most people would have missed it. But Cathy doesn't.

'Yes, she is.' Already she's said too much. She must stop now.

'Cathy, I'm going to get her back.'

Straight away, Cathy's heart starts thumping. But whose heart would not beat faster after hearing Jason say that. For he and Lauren belong together. And Jason is confiding in her; she can't help feeling a burst of pleasure about that.

'So tell me, Cathy,' his voice is driving her right to the edge of telling him. But then she takes one step backwards.

'Answer me this first, Jason,' she says. 'Did you send Lauren those flowers and cards?'

'What flowers and cards?'

'Oh, you know,' cries Cathy. 'You know. Come on, tell me.'

171

He doesn't answer her.

'Jason.'

The silence just stretches on and on. He's rung off, hasn't he?

But then she hears him declare, 'I'm never buying a red rose again, three pounds seventy five p each they cost me. Talk about a rip-off.'

Now it's Cathy who doesn't speak. There are no words to express how happy she feels. Of course it was Jason. It had to be him. How could she ever have doubted, but it was so unlike him. He's never sent a girl flowers in his life. So for him to do that for Lauren shows . . .

'Oh, Jason, if you were standing beside me now I'd hug you.'

'Lucky I'm not then,' there's that little crack in his voice again. He's really embarrassed about those roses, isn't he?

Then she says, 'Lauren and Grant are going to a party at Swanks on Friday night. That's where Lauren is planning to tell Grant that she doesn't want to see him any more. It's an exclusive party, so they might not let you in.'

'I'll get in,' growls Jason. 'By the way, thanks, Cathy.'

It's quite unusual to hear Jason thank anyone. Cathy savours the moment.

'Don't tell Lauren I'll be going, will you? I want it to be a surprise.'

'No, all right.'

'And you've not to tell anyone about the roses EVER. Promise.'

She smiles. 'Promise.' Then she asks, 'Just what are you actually going to do? I don't think Lauren will want any trouble.'

'There won't be any trouble,' says Jason briskly. 'Trust me.'

And before Cathy can ask him anything else, he's rung off.

# 7 Can't Help Falling in Love

Adam's party is over. And it's been a strange evening, Cathy thinks. This is the first birthday party Adam's had since Lisa died but everything was just as Cathy remembered. Well, the food certainly was: smoked salmon bagels, chopped herrings, pickled cucumbers and another wonderful honey cake. The cider flowed as usual too – when they were younger Adam's parents were the only ones who served alcohol – and this time there was also wine, most of which Lauren consumed, her eyes growing huger after every glass.

But despite this, everything seemed rather strained. Mark certainly was very quiet, sitting back in his chair, tapping his fingers on the table as if he couldn't wait to leave, while his 'girlfriend', Becky, was on his left, her hair up in a tight bun, her face glistening with sweat.

And then Jason was mysteriously late. The party did come alive when he arrived and with Jez formed a kind of comic double-act. But even so, Cathy felt everyone was relieved when the meal was over. Now they could go on to the karaoke party at The White Hart.

But first there's one last ceremony to be performed by Jason. He saunters across Adam's driveway and immediately the dark night is lit by warning flashlights. Only tonight, they are spotlights: Jason even turns and gives a brief salute to his audience, clustered around the doorway. Cathy expects Adam to follow him. But he doesn't. And it is his new motorbike which is being inspected.

Jason walks around the motorbike. It's green with touches of pink and, earlier, everyone else had pronounced it 'very flash'. But this is the verdict that counts. As usual, on these occasions, Jason's face betrays no emotion whatsoever. Next he bends down and peers at the speedometer. '80' he announces to no one in particular.

Finally he sits on the bike, revving up the engine for what seems, to Cathy, like several days before declaring, 'This is one of the best bikes on the road.' Adam's face is one huge smile now as he rushes forward, crash helmet in hand, closely followed by Mark. Becky and Jez saunter behind them. Cathy and Lauren watch them from the doorway.

175

'Phew, what a relief, Jason likes it.' Lauren's voice is lightly sarcastic. Then she says, 'Will it always be like this, Cathy. When we're in our eighties, will Jason be inspecting our walking frames?'

Cathy laughs. 'Can you imagine Jason old? I can't. But one day I suppose he will be like my grandad, stooped and bald with his blue eyes all pale and watery and sinking into his head.'

'Jason will never get old,' says Lauren firmly. 'He'll be the one person who won't. We'll all get old, though. I certainly will. I'm getting old now. I can't believe how rough I look tonight.'

For as long as Cathy's known Lauren, she's been exclaiming about how she's losing her looks. But this time, although she certainly doesn't look rough, there are dark lines under her eyes which Lauren has tried to cover up with so much make-up, she's actually made it worse.

Cathy guesses that all this gossip and the spiteful behaviour of some of the girls at college has been getting Lauren down more than she lets on. And it isn't really surprising. What's really annoying is how everyone at college is acting as if Lauren seduced Grant. When it's he who's done all the running. And he who is forcing Lauren to keep seeing him. But not after tomorrow night. Cathy knows Lauren's really determined about that.

'You don't look rough at all, Lauren,' says Cathy. 'Honestly.' Lauren gives her a little squeeze. 'And

I've been such a piglet this evening. Now I need to lose a stone by tomorrow. Do you think that's too ambitious?' She laughs and sways slightly. 'And I need to lose it all around my hips.'

'Do you still feel cold?' asks Cathy. Earlier, Lauren had said she couldn't seem to get warm.

'Yes, I do. I reckon I've got frostbite from opening my fridge door so often and wondering what I can put my lips around next.' Lauren laughs again. But Cathy can't help noticing that Lauren does look distinctly shivery.

'By the way, Cathy, your new dress really suits you,' says Lauren. 'Ask anyone.' She looks up to see Jez stomping over to them. 'Cathy's new dress, what do you think, Jez?' she calls.

Jez appraises Cathy for a moment. 'Have you still got the receipt?'

'Why?' exclaims Cathy, then she sees him smiling into his beard.

'No, blue is your colour,' he says, 'goes with your eyes.'

Cathy doesn't say anything. Everyone's been paying her compliments tonight. But she's not sure if they're just being kind.

Jez studies Lauren. 'Are you all right?'

Lauren sighs. 'Oh, I'm just wonderful.'

'I'm all packed,' he goes on. He makes it sound as if he's off on his hols, Cathy thinks. In a way, she supposes he is.

'I still don't understand why you're going,' says Cathy. 'And it's all been so sudden. First of all Jez had a new job on a flower stall and was telling everyone how much he was looking forward to it. Unfortunately, Jez was sacked after one morning, because he asked this old lady if she'd like her daffodils 'in a bag' or were they to 'eat now'.

The old lady wasn't amused and neither was Jez's boss.

But Jez was laughing when he told Cathy about it and said he wasn't bothered by the sacking at all. The following day Jez rang Cathy to tell her he'd had enough of Cartford and was, 'shooting back to Berlin again, for a spell'.

'Jez, exactly why are you leaving us?' asks Lauren.

Jez explains. 'That's the whole joy of being semi-retired, Lauren. You don't have to take your holidays when the bosses tell you. You can take off whenever you like.'

'In the end you'll have to get a job, though,' says Lauren.

'Oh I don't mind doing a few hours in the Hall of Cards or something. But I never want to do the same job every day. All that hassle, all that bureaucracy, all that competition, which isn't natural and just brings out the nasty side of people. No, I'm just one of Cartford's floating surplus of workers. But instead of floating around Cartford, I'm floating round the world instead.'

'So long as you come back,' says Cathy.

All of a sudden, Jason revs up the engine again. Adam hands him his crash helmet and then Jason tears off out of sight. Mark and Adam stay on the drive talking, while Becky walks up to the house.

'Where's Jason off to?' Cathy asks Becky.

'Adam insisted he take it out for a test run,' says Becky, with a wry smile.

Lauren looks at her watch. 'If he doesn't hurry up we're going to miss the start of the karaoke.' She shivers. 'Oh, well, it's freezing out here, so we'd better go back inside. Which is a bit embarrassing when we've just said thank you and goodnight to Adam's mum.'

Becky follows them inside, taking one last look at Adam and Mark. They've been boring her rigid with all this talk of 'getting wheels'.

Still, for the first time in ages Adam and Mark seem really relaxed together. That's why she's left them on their own. Maybe now they can get on to discussing what's really bugging them: her. She feels distinctly guilty about all this tension between them and she's keen for them to be friends again, like they were, B.B. (Before Becky). But the problem as she sees it is that neither Adam nor Mark will talk things out. Get everything out in the open, she advised Adam. For the things you don't say grow bigger and bigger until you can't see over the top of them any more. That's what went wrong with her parents.

So, as she left them, she gave Adam one of her significant looks. This was to remind him to thank Mark for agreeing to play her boyfriend again. She can't believe Adam hasn't done that yet. He said it was too embarrassing. But all he's got to say is thank you to his best friend. Surely it can't be that difficult.

Becky is about to follow the others into the dining room when she has an idea: she'll go and ask Mrs Rosen if she needs any help with the washing-up. Parents like it if you do things like that. Also, up to now, she doesn't feel she's made a terribly good impression. But she's been so nervous. Yet, even though she and Mrs Rosen are going to end up as deadly enemies, she also wants Mrs Rosen to think she's a nice girl.

She's not sure if she should knock on the kitchen door. Is that too formal? In the end she gives a quick knock, the kind her mum gives before entering her bedroom.

Mrs Rosen is scraping the leftovers into a bin bag. Even though they'd all eaten plenty, there was still masses left over.

'Oh, hi,' says Becky. 'Do you want a hand?'

Mrs Rosen looks startled. 'That's very kind of you dear, but it won't take me long. And Mr

Rosen'll be home any minute, so I shall be volunteering him to help.'

They both exchange tiny smiles. Then Mrs Rosen says, 'Are they still playing with Adam's bike?' She makes it sound as if they're about seven.

'Yes, that's right, they love that bike, don't they?'

'I told Adam he'd got to go for lessons every Sunday before we'll let him go very far,' says Mrs Rosen. And Becky senses Mrs Rosen is anxious about Adam on that bike. She feels a stab of sympathy for her. She knows exactly what Mrs Rosen's fears are. She shares them.

'Mark, he's a nice boy, isn't he?' says Mrs Rosen suddenly.

'Oh, yes, he is. Very nice.'

'Known him for years, of course. A good boy and a good friend to Adam, but one who can be hurt.' Her eyes narrow as she says this. Becky is startled. Why did she say that? But now Mrs Rosen is smiling faintly again. 'Anyway, dear, thank you for your very kind offer. I'll see you again, no doubt.'

Oh, yes, thinks Becky, you're going to see a great deal more of me. But she says nothing and closes the kitchen door behind her. She hears Lauren's laugh coming from the dining room. She is about to go in, when, on impulse, she turns and opens the lounge door, which had been tightly and mysteriously closed all the time they'd been there.

181

It's what her mum would call a heavy room. A gold lamp in the corner sends a pale, tentative light over a chaise longue, a thick carpet and lots of elderly furniture. What they need in here, decides Becky, is a nice white rug and some pictures on the walls and a blazing log fire. There's too much furniture in here too. In fact, they've more furniture in here than she and her mum have in the whole of their downstairs.

She peers in at the glass cabinet: those candlesticks must be the ones Adam said are lit on Fridays. And that silver wine goblet, Adam's mentioned that too, hasn't he? She scrutinises the books on the shelves: they're all blue leather jobs. In fact, they look just like her mum's set of Dickens. But actually, they're prayer books. And then at the end of the shelf are two large framed photographs, one is of a boy who Becky guesses is Adam's brother. The other is of Adam himself.

Becky's mother won't have photographs on display in the house. She says, 'All photographs do is remind you how cruel time is. Every photograph in the world ends up sad.' Becky disagrees with her. Yet, right now, as she takes down Adam's photograph, she feels a sadness as heavy as this room.

For in the photograph, Adam's got a little cap on his head and a shawl round his shoulders. This is obviously his *barmitzvah* picture. And doesn't he look serious? As if this all really matters to him. And perhaps it does. Suddenly, she feels afraid. This is the part of Adam she can never share.

'And what are you doing?' growls a deep unfamiliar voice. Becky nearly drops the picture with fright. Then she spins round expecting to see Adam's father, spluttering with rage, and instead sees Adam grinning away at her.

'Don't do that,' she cries. He starts laughing.

'It's not funny,' she says. 'I was wetting myself.' She holds up the picture.

'Don't I look a right stiff,' says Adam.

'Is it your *barmitzvah* picture?' she asks. He nods.

'And what's that cap?'

'It's called the skull cap.'

'And that shawl?'

'The prayer shawl. Go on, put it away,' he says.

'No, it's interesting.'

'No, it's not. It was a very long time ago anyway.' He sounds a little cross, so she carefully puts the picture back. He says, 'How I hated this room.'

'Why?'

'Well, whenever you came in here it was always, don't sit on the sofa in your dirty jeans, don't lean back, we don't want hair on the sofa . . .' The bitterness that had crept into his voice vanishes. 'It's great suddenly seeing you in here.' He sits down on the sofa. 'Come on, join me.'

'Say your mother . . .'

'She won't. She'll be in the kitchen for hours.'

She sits down on the edge of the chaise longue. She's never seen one in a house before, only in films, where ladies seemed to recline on them eating grapes.

'It's like sitting on a stone, isn't it?' he says.

'No, not quite as comfortable as that.' Then she asks, 'What happened with Mark?'

'Don't ask.'

'Why, come on. Tell me.'

'Well, I thanked him for coming today as your boyfriend, just like you ordered me,' he smiles briefly, 'and straight away he went up like a rocket, shouting at me about how he was getting a girl-friend of his own any day. He just went on and on. I couldn't stop him. In the end I wanted to punch him, he got me that mad. But then I thought, this is my best mate, the guy who stood by me so many times, the guy who arranged for us to go out together. Yet, out there, he was like a madman, swearing at me. And in the end he just walked off. Lauren and Cathy have gone to find him. But I couldn't take any more.' He shakes his head. 'The trouble is, whenever I'm with him I feel guilty. Like I've cheated him.'

Becky gets up. 'No, it's me who should feel guilty. This is all my fault. I've caused you so much hassle with your family, your best friend,' she sways slightly. The room's musty smell is suddenly over-powering. 'I'm so sorry,' she cries.

And then all at once Adam is standing over her. 'No, no,' he's practically shouting. He pulls her to him. 'You're the best thing that's ever happened to me,' he says it so fiercely, it's almost comic. 'And I'm never going to let you go.'

She stares at him in his brown jacket, the white shirt she'd bought him, grey trousers, with his hair well slicked back and showing off his finely chiselled features. And, finally, there are those dark eyes, full of sadness. He needs her so badly, doesn't he? That's why she must never let him down.

He waves a gloved hand at her. 'Thank you for my gloves.' These are her secret birthday present to him. He reaches into his jacket pocket. 'This is for you, by the way.' He brings out a small parcel.

'You shouldn't be giving me presents on your birthday,' says Becky. 'But I'll rip it open anyway.' Inside is a little box containing a ring. A gold ring.

'It's nothing too amazing,' says Adam, 'more of a classic ring, I suppose. One you can keep for a long time.'

'Oh, it's wonderful.' Her voice has gone all breathy. If angels exist, they'll have voices just like that. She pulls all the rings off her left hand. 'They're all really cheap rings really, thin and tacky. I think this one cost me fifty p.' Then she starts

185

on her right hand. 'From now on I shall only wear one ring,' she says.

'Well, that ring is just like a first instalment,' says Adam. Now his arms are around her waist and his lips surge on to hers. She feels herself drawing closer and closer to him, then abruptly pulls away again as a door clicks open and Mrs Rosen stares across at them.

'Your friends are looking for you,' she says, flatly. 'They are ready to leave now.'

'Oh, right, thanks Mum,' says Adam, his voice muffled. She closes the door noiselessly behind her.

'Do you think she saw us?' asks Becky.

'Yes,' says Adam, slowly. 'I think she did.'

'Will she say anything?' asks Becky.

'Probably not at first,' he frowns, but then says, 'So what. I don't care if she does. In fact, I almost want her to know. For she can't break us up now, no one can.'

'Look, there's Mark,' cries Cathy.

Becky knew he wouldn't have gone home, as they'd all been saying. And she'd guessed he'd be here. He is sitting outside The White Hart, surrounded on all sides by empty tables. Inside, the pub music can already be heard.

'Look, you go on,' says Becky. 'I'll talk to Mark.'

'Do you want me . . .' begins Adam.

'No, it's all right,' says Becky.

She walks quickly up to Mark's table. He is slouched forward, with one hand pressing on to his face.

'Hi, Mark.' He doesn't answer. 'Aren't you cold?' she asks. He shrugs his shoulders. She sits down opposite him. He still doesn't look at her. 'In a mood?'

'No, not at all.' Now he's looking at her.

'Adam said you had a bit of a go at him.'

'Adam said,' he mimics.

'Did Adam say something to annoy you? Come on, Mark tell me.'

Mark puts his hand down. There's a large red mark on his face now.

'Adam didn't say anything at all. Everything he said was you talking through him, wasn't it? For I know how Adam talks, and that wasn't him. All that apology crap was you, wasn't it?'

Before Becky can reply Mark rushes on. 'And I find that really insulting.'

'You do?'

'Yes, I do. You don't control Adam and me, you know.'

'I know.'

He pauses for a second, then says, 'I knew right away you were behind it.'

'I don't think this has been one of my better

days,' says Becky, sadly. 'I shouldn't have interfered – you're right.'

'You probably meant well,' concedes Mark.

'Oh, yes, I always mean well,' says Becky. 'But everything's such a muddle. Adam's mum saw us together in the lounge.'

'Doing what?'

'Kissing.'

'Shit,' he almost whistles the word.

'Exactly.'

'Did she say anything?'

'No, but she's probably thinking a lot.'

'Is Adam, worried?'

'No, he says he wants her to know. So I don't know what he'll do.'

She stretches out her hand to him. He gently takes it, then says, 'Your rings have gone.'

'Yeah.'

'They've all gone, except for . . . that's new, isn't it, Adam?'

'Yes.'

He stares down at the table, then asks, 'Everyone else gone inside?'

'Yes.'

'Better go in then, hadn't we?'

'Mark.' She wants to tell him how much she values his friendship. But if she says this now, will it sound as if she's handing Mark a consolation prize? You can't go out with me but you do take away the glittering runners-up prize: being my special friend. It's true and yet it cannot help sound counterfeit and patronising. So in the end she just takes his hand again. This time, he clasps it tightly.

Adam is hovering inside the entrance of The White Hart. As soon as Mark sees him, he releases his hand from Becky. They stare at each other for a long moment. Then Mark says, 'This place has changed a bit, hasn't it?'

Adam immediately picks up the conversational tone. 'Yeah, this used to be a real old man's pub, didn't it?'

'I remember you and me walking in here once,' says Mark, 'and right away the guy behind the bar goes, "Now we don't want any gangs in here."' He grins. 'Now look at it.'

Walking into the old White Hart had been like walking into someone's house, with its large, ugly chairs, its curtains and its dim, little red lampshades: a place of endless nooks and crannies; of corners claimed and guarded fiercely.

Now, the corners have all gone. The White 'under totally new management' Hart, is just one huge room; the kind you might hire to hold parties in.

Garishly bright posters of Superman, Sylvester Stallone and Coca Cola have taken over the walls, while crowds of young people surge around the

189

bar, to be served by even younger-looking people, all wearing blue shirts and red bow-ties.

Over in the corner, a woman with blonde hair reaching to her shoulders yells down a microphone, 'If you've just arrived, this is Rachel, welcoming you to the White Hart's Karaoke night.' She turns to the small crowd gathered around her, 'Are you enjoying yourselves?' Perhaps wisely, she doesn't wait for a reply. 'All rightie. Now I know you're going to give a really big welcome to Cartford's two wild, crazy men of rock, Les and Steve.' Les and Steve, looking about as wild and crazy as The Smurfs, huddle by the wall, while stumbling their way through 'Should I stay or Should I go' Mark watches them carefully. 'They're not putting any life into it,' he observes.

Then Adam says, 'We're at the back,' and leads Mark and Becky over to a large table at which Jez and Lauren are slumped, while coats and bags guard the other seats.

Adam immediately moves one of the large heavy chairs back a little and then says, gently, 'Becky.' She flushes both with embarrassment and pleasure. Adam's good manners can still take her by surprise. Mark sits down on her other side.

'Jason insisted on getting the drinks,' explained Jez. 'And Cathy's helping him.'

'So what acts have we missed?' asks Becky.

'The Stone Roses. Pink Floyd . . .' begins Jez.

'Oh, nothing much then,' replies Becky.

'New ring?' asks Lauren, leaning forward.

'Yes, Adam bought it for me,' says Becky.

Lauren nods. 'Very nice.'

'The boys have finished,' bawls Rachel from the stage. 'So you can clap now.'

Loud applause from the boys' mates and distinctly scattered applause from everyone else follows.

'Marks out of ten please for Les and Steve,' asks Jez.

'Minus five,' says Lauren.

'One for courage,' says Adam.

Cathy bobs over, 'Jason's got your usual Mark, but wasn't sure what you wanted Becky?'

'Oh, I'll just have an orange and lemonade,' says Becky.

'Becky's not drinking as she's going to give us a song in a minute,' says Jez.

'No way,' cries Becky 'I've got the worst voice in the world. 'It's Mark who can sing.' But Mark doesn't react to this.

Cathy returns to the bar. 'Becky just wants an orange and lemonade, Jason.'

Jason repeats this information to the girl behind the bar, adding, 'And of course, whatever you're having, Helen.'

'Oh thank you Jason,' the girl behind the bar gives him a broad smile. Then Jason nods at two guys who walk past. 'I reckon just about everyone in here must know me,' he says.

'I know I feel really honoured to be allowed to stand beside you,' mocks Cathy.

'And so you should be.' Jason smiles. And it's hard to say which gleams whiter: Jason's white shirt or his teeth.

'Were you able to get an invite to Swanks tomorrow?'

'But of course.'

Cathy can't help but be impressed. 'So how did you manage that. For you're not exactly a local V.I.P. yet. Are you darlin'?'

Jason is shocked. 'Yes I am.'

'Come on, tell me. Did your boss at the sports shop get you in?'

'Well, yes,' he concedes unwillingly. 'Something like that. By the way, Cathy,' Jason's voice is suddenly low and confiding, as if he's about to give her some top secret information. 'Lauren does want to finish with this gremlin, doesn't she?'

Cathy is stunned he should even ask her such a question. Surely it's obvious to anyone how unhappy Lauren is. 'Yes she does. Definitely. Why do you ask?'

'I don't know,' his voice is so low now, Cathy can hardly hear him. It's just I was expecting this Grant to be some polyester-jacketed, acne-faced, specky git, who still wears Y-fronts and instead he . . . Well, he wouldn't come last in a John Lennon lookalike contest, would he?'

Cathy's shocked. Jason is Mr Confidence, or that's the mask he wears so successfully. Only right now that mask is full of holes.

'I swear to you, Lauren has no interest in Grant at all.'

'Yeah, well, I knew that really,' says Jason. 'But thanks.'

'I suppose you can't tell me what you're planning to do tomorrow night?'

'I regret I cannot divulge my plans at this stage,' says Jason. 'But I think you'll be pleased, Cathy.' The mask is back in place now. But it's a much thinner mask than Cathy ever suspected, or it is where Lauren is concerned anyway.

Back at the table Jason proposes a birthday toast to Adam, then declares, 'It is with great relief, I mean regret, that I note the passing of Jez from Cartford. Before committing him to foreign parts, I think we should drink a toast to Jez – and may his beard never fall out.'

'To Jez,' everyone repeats. Jez stumbles to his feet. 'What can I say, except when I'm in Berlin I shall think longingly of tonight and all this wonderful music,' (he points to the stage where two girls are currently screeching their way through *Summer Nights*) 'and the pub's glorious decor.' He makes a face at the American posters, 'And of course my friends. So anyway, here's to you, here's to me, here's to us.' Everyone stands up now, glasses clink together and as they sit down again Adam notices Becky's jacket has fallen to the floor. He immediately bends down and picks it up.

'Brush it down carefully, Adam,' mutters Lauren.

Cathy nudges her, 'Don't be wicked.'

'But look at the two of them, talk about super-glue.'

'They're in love, Lauren.'

'Tell me about it,' says Lauren, with a laugh. Then she hisses, 'Seen the ring Adam's bought her?'

'Not jealous, are you?'

'Definitely,' says Lauren. 'How about you?'

Rachel's voice is yelling, 'Thank you girls, remind me not to let you sing along again. Only joking. Now singing *Crazy for You* is Vanessa.' But no one surfaces into view. Then a voice calls, 'She's gone home.' 'No bottle, eh?' cries Rachel. 'Well, we don't care, do we folks? Come on, speak to me, or are you all dead out there?'

'You should never insult your audience,' mutters Mark. 'She should know that.'

Rachel's voice splutters over the microphone, 'Next then, we have Gary, singing *Nights in White Satin*. So come on Justin, I mean Gary.'

There's a sound of a scuffle by the loo, then someone yelling, 'He's locked himself in.'

'What's everyone so afraid of,' asks Rachel. 'I don't bite you know. Well, not much. Now, ladies and gentlemen, it appears we have a gap in the entertainment. So now's the chance for some lucky person who's not on my list to show me their talent. I think I'd better re-phrase that.' She laughs into the microphone, her voice sounding increasingly hoarse. 'Any lady or gentleman who thinks they have a talent for singing, now's your chance to be discovered. Who knows, there might even be some record producers in the audience. So come on, roll up.'

'Mark, why don't you go up,' says Jason.

'No way,' snaps Mark.

'Go on,' presses Jason, 'You're miles better than these peasants.'

'No,' repeats Mark, but not quite so fervently.

'Yeah, go on Mark,' chorus Becky and Lauren.

'Lots of lovely girls in tonight,' murmurs Jason. 'Just saw Tania over there.' Then before Mark can reply, Jason calls out, 'Mark'll do it.'

'Mark,' the compere leaps gratefully on to the name. 'Where are you Mark?'

'Go on,' says Jason. It's practically an order. Mark slowly gets to his feet and then, is pushed forward.

'Come on, ladies and gentlemen, let's give Mark

some encouragement, shall we?' Light applause follows Mark as he makes the long journey up to the stage. Into his head flash images from old gangster films of men making that last walk to the executioner. Now he knows how they felt. Then, he is enveloped by a smell of cigarettes and sweat as Rachel puts her arms around him. 'Mmm, he's quite nice girls, just my size. Got a good voice, have you Mark?'

'Not bad,' he mutters, his throat suddenly, alarmingly dry. What is he doing up here?'

'Pick a song from the list, Mark?'

He scans the list, in a daze. He's up here in front of hundreds of people, about to make a complete fool of himself. He wonders if he should do a runner. Then, he sees Becky, Lauren and Cathy push their way through to the front. While speckled around him are people he knows from college. No, that would be even more embarrassing. Then, on the list, he sees the song he sings over and over in the bath. It's like seeing an old and trusted friend. He relaxes a little. 'I'll sing, *Can't Help Falling in Love,*' he says.

'An Elvis Presley classic,' she says, then points to the TV screen.

'Now you just follow the red dot for the words, like in the Ovaltine ads. Do you remember those?'

'Yes.'

'Well you're older than you look, aren't you?

196

Okay folks, let's have the lights down, for this is –
A – L O V E – song.'

'Come on, let's give him a bit of moral support,'
Lauren tells Cathy and Becky. And all three of
them immediately start clapping and yelling.

'You'll put him off,' mutters Jason, behind them.

'No we won't,' says Lauren. 'Come on, Mark,'
she cries again.

Now he just wants to get on with it. He's scared
but oddly excited too.

As soon as Mark starts singing, Becky stares at
him in amazement. For his singing voice is quite
husky, much deeper than his speaking voice. Why,
he's good. As the song goes on, Mark's voice grows
stronger, the words soaring out over the audience.
Becky looks round. Practically the whole pub is
gazing at Mark now. And there's quite a crowd
around him. Some couples start swaying in time
with the music, while a small pack of girls are
pushing their way through to the front.

Becky must have heard this song a hundred
times. But today's the first time she's really listened
to the words. She looks up. Mark is staring right
at her.

Then Mark carries his Elvis impersonation
further, by thrusting his pelvis at the audience, just
the once at first and a trifle tentatively, it must be
said. But the crowd immediately cheer and stamp
their feet. Mark, encouraged, performs the pelvis

thrusting again, this time, with considerably more energy. By the end, the pub is one giant roar of applause.

Mark gazes into the audience with undisguised delight. He's brought the whole pub together. For one brief, glorious moment, there are no outsiders. He's lifted people up to another plane, where all the petty aggressions are forgotten. The plane where we all should live.

'Look at him just lapping it up,' says Lauren fondly.

'Ah, I knew you were out there,' cries Rachel, beaming at the audience. She turns to Mark, 'May I touch you?' She pats him on the bottom, then rolls her eyes at the girls in the front. Are you single, Mark?'

'Yes,' he says. His speaking voice suddenly as deep as his singing one.

'Well, we can't let him go without an encore, can we?' The crowd roar their agreement. 'So here he is ladies and gentlemen, Cartford's own hunky, chunk of burning gold funk . . .'

Cathy smiles around at Adam and Jason, then notices Jez is missing.

'Where's Jez?' she asks.

'He's gone,' says Jason, 'said he couldn't think of a better note to leave on. He wanted to just slip away.'

'But he can't just leave like that,' cries Cathy. 'How long ago did he go?'

'About a minute ago, when Mark finished.'

Cathy is immediately jostling her way throught the crowd.

'Goodnight, come again,' cries the grinning bouncer on the door. But Cathy doesn't even see him. She races outside. It's drizzling with rain and the sky is a fierce black colour. Even so, she can quickly make out Jez at the top of the road.

'Jez,' she calls. He immediately turns round. She pants over to him. 'What's the idea of sneaking off like that?'

'I hate goodbyes,' he says.

The sounds of *Can't Help Falling in Love* waft towards them.

'Mark's doing an encore,' explains Cathy.

'He was just brilliant, wasn't he?' says Jez, his face briefly lighting up. 'And Jason and Lauren have been cyeing each other all evening. Do you think they're going to get back together?'

'I think there's a good chance,' says Cathy. 'I'll write and let you know, provided you write back more regularly than last time.' Her voice is suddenly stern, like a teacher reminding a class of holiday assignments.

'I'll do my best. I'm just such a totally disorganised person – and very lazy.' He stops. 'I'm pausing for you to disagree with me.'

Cathy laughs, then asks, 'You don't need any money, do you?'

'No, I'm okay, I've still got a bit left from my pay-off at Radleys and I scrounged some from my dad and Jason. So I've got enough to go to Berlin and buy a cup of coffee when I get there.' He gives a mirthless laugh. 'Don't really know why I'm going back. To tell you the truth, I think I just like getting on planes. I've never been able to see a plane without wishing I was on it. Still, going off like this is a cop-out really; doesn't show much strength of character, all that stuff. Next time I come back, as my old maths teacher would say, I'll "get down to it" and go and work in an office and become a turd with a tie.'

'Oh, don't ever do that,' exclaims Cathy.

'No, okay, But maybe when I come back I'll find out what my thing is. I doubt if it will be work, though,' he adds.

'Perhaps you'll open that sweet shop.'

'Yeah, and you'll have converted us all into vegetarians.'

'It's happening already,' cries Cathy. 'We've had masses of enquiries since the Radleys demo. And we're organising another this month. Now I know why you're leaving.'

'That's it. No, really, I sort of admire the way you keep pushing away and hitting all those poor people out there. Good stuff. Even though we never had that meal together, did we? You turned me down, remember.'

'You only asked me the once,' replies Cathy. 'And I couldn't get out of that meeting.'

'Gave up too soon, did I?' says Jez, mockingly.

The sound of applause is ringing behind them now.

'Thanks to Mark, it's really kicking in there now, isn't it?' says Jez. 'I'd better go. Cathy, look after yourself, won't you?'

He gives her a hug, then looks as if he is going to say something else. But in the end, he just waves, before disappearing into the night.

Lauren switches her hair dryer off. What's her dad shouting about now? Then she decides he must be rowing with her mum again. Last month Dad bought her mother a Mercedes sports car as a reward for losing weight. Only, ever since she got the sports car, Mum has started putting on weight again. So this morning she opened the garage door to find her Mercedes sports car transformed into an old banger.

Dad was really tough about it too, at first. He said Mum hadn't kept her side of the bargain so he wasn't keeping his side either. A deal was a deal. But then Mum went on the offensive, backed up by Lauren, and now Dad's saying it's all a joke, and the Mercedes will be returned tomorrow. Mum's not letting up on him yet, though.

Lauren smiles to herself. Still, at least their antics have distracted her away from who's waiting for her in less than an hour now. She's about to switch the hair dryer back on when she hears Dad trumpeting away again. Only this time she's sure she hears her name. He's trumpeting at her quite a lot lately. Especially when she told him about the incident in the library. She said it was a practical joke that had gone wrong. They both took her side and he's going up to the college on Monday. She's dreading it.

She hurls the hair dryer down and rushes downstairs. Her dad is standing in the kitchen and glaring at her. 'At last,' he says. 'Didn't you hear me calling you?'

'No, I was drying my hair.'

'I thought you must still be in the bath. There was someone on the phone, most anxious to talk to you.'

'Who?'

'I don't know. I didn't get the name.'

'Oh, Dad,' cries Lauren. 'What use is that. Look, I put up a note about what to do when there's a call for me.' Just above the telephone pad, is a photocopied sheet of paper on which is written, *When there's a call for Lauren:*

202

1) *Ask who it is. Write the name down. Get them to spell it if necessary.*
2) *Then say I'm not sure if she's in or out.*
3) *Put the hand over the receiver and ask me if I'm in.*

'You've got to follow the procedure,' says Lauren.

'It's certainly not much use if you don't get the caller's name,' adds her mum, walking past them, over to the kettle.

'Now I remember,' says her dad, 'he didn't give a name, just said to remind you that he'll pick you up at seven o'clock.'

GRANT, thinks Lauren at once. But how dare he ring her at home. She'd told him he must *never* do that. And to think of him actually talking to her father. If her dad ever found out, well, she'd have to leave home. She just couldn't bear it.

'It was a man's voice,' says her father, 'a mature man's voice. I thought you were going to a party with Cathy tonight.'

Her mum puts down the kettle she was filling and walks over to Lauren.

'Oh, yes, that's right, I am going out with Cathy,' says Lauren, quickly. 'Only this friend, Grant, is giving us a lift. He and his girlfriend, Annabel, that is.' She knows this last sentence will ease their minds. 'I expect he was just checking I knew the time.'

'Oh well, that was kind of him,' says her mother.

'Wasn't it?' murmurs Lauren, before rushing back upstairs. She stands staring out of her window. The wind is howling outside, while the trees are shaking about like demented disco dancers. It's going to be a horrible night.

She switches on the radio to drown out the noise and begins brushing her hair. She still can't believe Grant rang up like that. He's acting as if he's about fifteen and going out with his first girlfriend. He must be really anxious that she's not going to turn up.

She should have ended this at college, shouldn't she. Only there never seemed a moment when they could talk, without a hundred unfriendly eyes looking on. And anyway, she thought of college as his territory. Oh, what a mess.

'Now, what lessons can we learn from this?' She suddenly hears her headmaster's voice in her head. He's always ask that question after telling one of his little stories in assembly, after which would come the great thundering moral.

So what moral would he draw from this. He'd draw his gown around his shoulders, then declare, 'Lauren tried to use Grant. She never considered him as a person, just as a means of getting taken to places she'd never been to before. And now Lauren is right out of her depth. And it's all her own bloody fault.' Except he wouldn't swear of course. Perish the thought.

Lauren slams the brush down. What does he know? It's not her fault, is it? She looks at her watch. It's nearly time to go. She'd better just check she's got enough money in her purse for a taxi home. She'd rather get a taxi anyway. And there in the purse she pulls out a picture of Jason. She stole it from him on their first ever date together. He suddenly said, 'Want to see a picture of me with spikey hair,' and showed her this snapshot of him when he was about eleven. And he's smiling – and not this Mr Cool smile but a really sweet, goofy grin. Lauren immediately loved it and slipped it into her purse, where it's remained ever since. Jason never asked for it back. Perhaps he never missed it.

Jason – how many weeks together did we have? And then we didn't even speak for a year. How could we have thrown away all that time. That certainly wasn't her fault. Jason hurt her deeply. Even now she can taste the anger she felt on the night of her fifteenth birthday, when she rubbed his name off their sacred scroll.

But how mean, how spiteful, that act seems now. Thank goodness he never found out what she'd done. Oh, Jason, we've wasted so much time. Suddenly, like a tune you can't get out of your head, her headmaster's voice pops up again. 'Now if

Lauren had given Jason a chance to explain and if she hadn't been so concerned with her pride, she wouldn't be in this muddle now. Pride comes before a fall, you know.'

'Go away,' cries Lauren. He's talking nothing but clichés anyway. Life isn't anywhere near as simple as he pretended in those rotten assemblies. Gently, carefully, she picks up Jason's picture and places it in the front of her purse. Then she looks at her watch. It's seven o'clock exactly. Grant'll be waiting for her now. She's sorely tempted not to go, to hide away in her room. But he'll only come looking for her. He'll knock on the door for her . . . The very thought makes her shudder violently.

She goes downstairs.

'Make sure you wear a coat tonight,' says her mum. 'And do you want this scarf, too? Your father bought it for me today, even though I've never worn a scarf in my life. And it's got horses on it and I hate horses. He knows that but he buys it anyway.'

'They're the in thing, aren't they, Lauren?' her dad's almost pleading.

'I think so,' says Lauren, 'but I won't wear it tonight, nice as it is,' she adds tactfully.

They wave her off from different sides of the hall. 'Take care,' calls her dad. 'It looks like a wild night.'

Sure enough, the wind is really building up now,

whistling and howling and generally behaving as if it were auditioning to be in the next horror film. Lauren lowers her head and starts walking down her drive, nearly colliding with Cathy.

'Cathy,' she cries. 'What are you doing here?'

'Just waiting to wish you luck.'

'Oh, Cathy, thank you,' says Lauren, touched. 'But why didn't you come in?'

'Well, I wasn't sure what story you'd told about tonight and I thought I'm bound to get it wrong.'

'Will you walk up a little way with me,' asks Lauren.

'Sure.' They link arms.

'I'm dreading this, you know,' says Lauren.

'Just be sure you tell him it's over,' says Cathy.

'Oh look, there he is.' Lauren points ahead of her.

Then Cathy says, 'Lauren, I wanted to say that if by chance something should happen tonight, something that you've wanted to happen . . . you will . . . you will . . . Oh, I don't know what I'm talking about.'

'Neither do I,' says Lauren. They stop walking. 'What are you trying to say?'

'Nothing. I'm just talking rubbish, as usual.'

'I don't suppose,' adds Cathy, 'that you'll be up before I go to work tomorrow. But you will ring me at The Record Room, though, won't you?'

'I'll tell you everything,' whispers Lauren, with

a pale smile. She squeezes Cathy's arm. 'Talk to you tomorrow, then.'

Cathy watches Lauren slowly walk to Grant's car. Then she suddenly calls out. 'Give me a ring tonight, no matter how late. I'll be up.'

Don't miss *Friends Forever III: Discovery* on sale March 1992.

What happens when JASON meets LAUREN and GRANT at Swanks?
Is it a happy ending for Jason and Lauren at last?

What about ADAM and BECKY?
Do Adam's parents discover their secret?

And why does CATHY run away from home?

And which character has to make the most important decision of his/her life . . . ?

*The story continues*

Pete Johnson

# ONE STEP BEYOND

Sometimes you're walking right on the edge
and don't even realise it.
Like Alex. He's waited five years to take
revenge on Mr Stones.
And Natasha. She's always done what her parents tell her – until the day she turns sixteen.
Then there's Yorga. He has a brilliant idea to
stop the hated Casuals taking over his town.
Just three of the people who don't realise
they're right on the edge – until they take one
step beyond.
A collection of eight dazzling stories of love,
revenge, laughter and horror.

"Pete Johnson, an author who can pinpoint
what is distinctive about his readers . . . without being either patronising or strait-jacketed
by their demands."

*Sunday Times*

# A selected list of title available from Teens · Mandarin

While every effort is made to keep prices low, it is sometimes necessary to increase prices at short notice. Mandarin Paperbacks reserves the right to show new retail prices on covers which may differ from those previously advertised in the text or elsewhere.

The prices shown below were correct at the time of going to press.

| | | | | |
|---|---|---|---|---|
| ☐ | 7497 0009 2 | **The Secret Diary of Adrian Mole Aged 13¾** | Sue Townsend | £2.50 |
| ☐ | 7497 0101 3 | **The Growing Pains of Adrian Mole** | Sue Townsend | £2.50 |
| ☐ | 7497 0018 1 | **Behind the Bike Sheds** | Jan Needle | £2.25 |
| ☐ | 416 10352 9 | **Lexie** | Mary Hooper | £1.99 |
| ☐ | 416 08282 3 | **After Thursday** | Jean Ure | £1.99 |
| ☐ | 416 10192 5 | **A Tale of Time City** | Diana Wynne-Jones | £1.99 |
| ☐ | 416 07442 1 | **Howl's Moving Castle** | Diana Wynne-Jones | £1.95 |
| ☐ | 416 08822 8 | **The Changeover** | Margaret Mahy | £1.95 |
| ☐ | 416 13102 6 | **Frankie's Story** | Catherine Sefton | £1.99 |
| ☐ | 416 11962 X | **Teens Book of Love Stories** | Miriam Hodgeson | £1.95 |
| ☐ | 416 12022 9 | **Picture Me Falling In Love** | June Foley | £1.99 |
| ☐ | 416 12612 X | **All the Fun of the Fair** | Anthony Masters | £2.25 |
| ☐ | 416 13862 4 | **Rough Mix** | Denis Bond | £1.99 |
| ☐ | 416 08082 0 | **Teenagers Handbook** | Murphy/Grime | £1.99 |

All these books are available at your bookshop or newsagent, or can be ordered direct from the publisher. Just tick the titles you want and fill in the form below.

**Mandarin Paperbacks**, Cash Sales Department, PO Box 11, Falmouth, Cornwall TR10 9EN.

Please send cheque or postal order, no currency, for purchase price quoted and allow the following for postage and packing:

| | |
|---|---|
| UK | 80p for the first book, 20p for each additional book ordered to a maximum charge of £2.00. |
| BFPO | 80p for the first book, 20p for each additional book. |
| Overseas including Eire | £1.50 for the first book, £1.00 for the second and 30p for each additional book thereafter. |

NAME (Block letters) ............................................................................................................

ADDRESS ............................................................................................................

............................................................................................................

............................................................................................................